Life's a Laughin' Matter

by

Jay Bernard

Editor: Roxane Christ

Bloomington, IN

Milton Keynes, UK

AuthorHouse™
1663 Liberty Drive, Suite 200
Bloomington, IN 47403
www.authorhouse.com
Phone: 1-800-839-8640

AuthorHouse™ UK Ltd.
500 Avebury Boulevard
Central Milton Keynes, MK9 2BE
www.authorhouse.co.uk
Phone: 08001974150

First published by AuthorHouse 2/14/2006

ISBN: 1-4259-1644-9 (sc)
ISBN: 1-4259-1643-0 (dj)

Printed in the United States of America
Bloomington, Indiana

This book is printed on acid-free paper.

Graphics by Lorriane Fee

Table of Contents

Sour Lemons 1
The Gift 7
Ralph's Jitney 11
Mighty White Hunters 15
Runaway! 19
Double Trouble 23
Identified Flying Objects 27
Mini Mechanic 31
Pregnant Idea 35
In The Clover 39
The Big Shot 43
Blessed be the Mouth 47
Nuts! 51
Porter Panic 55
Bee Line 59
Fingering It Out 65
Watermelon Whine 69
What's on Tap 73
Reserved Decision 77
Tanked 83
Gassed 87
Les is More 93
Run Chicken Run 97
Dialing Paws 101
Carnanigans 105
Southern Comfort 109

Makin' a Difference....111
It's New - Try It! 117
Board Lady....121
Cruisin' for Trouble....125
Night Light....129
Courting Miss Sarah....133
Sink or Swim....137
The Bear Facts....141
The Boxer....145
Sleepy Mechanic....149
Life Savers....155
Mocha Mo....161
Long Road Home....165
Kill 'Em with Kindness....169
Three Weddings - Two Grooms....173
The Earache....179
Painted Into a Corner....183
Dad's Treasure....187
Upper Deck....191
Soccer Champion....197
Bucket Head....201
Stealin' Time....205
Jeepers Creepers....209
About the Author....217

Sour Lemons

Harvest was in full swing on the little farm. It was Ben's favorite time of year beyond any doubt. Activity was at its height and there were many visitors with whom he could chat. Sure they were hired hands, but they had ventured west from across the country to help with the gathering of the crop. There was much to be learned as they spun tales of their experiences each evening. Nothing could be better.

Being a youngster he, of course, managed to avoid any work. His main responsibility was traipsing along with his mother as she delivered coffee and sandwiches to the field twice each day to ensure the harvest crew was fed and happy. This was a pleasure. During these times, he learned the most from the men in the field and was afforded an opportunity to decide which stories he'd like to hear a second time that evening.

Meeting the hungry crew at the close of the day was also exciting for the young boy. Each fall, he developed favorites among the men in the field and a short walk was sure to have him picked up to ride on one of the wagons. The horse drawn chariots did not really move at break-neck speed, but to Ben, it seemed fast as hay racks charged into the yard and men prepared for the evening meal. In addition, some of his favorites returned year after year, always with new stories of the saga of their lives.

Even the mornings were an event. Ben rose early, watched the horses hitched to the wagons and the men head for the fields. On many occasions, he would catch a ride and spend his morning riding atop bundles of grain. But this could only happen after breakfast and accomplishing his deeds of the day. First there were minimal chores, which needed doing as he began his training as a farmer followed by some personal accomplishments to add to his enjoyment. He had to steal away, like a thief in the night, gain his prize and deliver it to the cook's car where his older cousins struggled to feed the hungry crew.

Each morning, he waited for his mother to turn her back. When she was not paying attention, or pretended not to be, he would quietly steal a small pie plate; tuck it away beneath a jacket and head outdoors. A short trip to the cook's car, he would deliver the plate to one of his cousins and the deed was done. Now he could relax and enjoy the day, until early afternoon when it was time to return to the scene of his crime to collect his ill-gotten gains.

The arrival of the afternoon, again found him making his way to the cook's car to visit a cousin. He wanted his prize, his reward for the morning's work. He was never disappointed. He was inevitably greeted with a hot lemon meringue pie - his favorite. A quick trip to a tree stump out behind the barn and he had the entire treasure to himself. Hidden away in his quiet place was a fork, which he wiped after each excursion and wrapped carefully to avoid dirt, the world was his.

Ben didn't hide from everyone, however. His cousin Carol often came along with her mother in the mornings and, if she was present, he had no problem sharing his treasure. He felt a closeness for Carol that exceeded that of his other cousins, even the bakers. With her, he would always share. They shared a great deal more than pies, however. As a pair, they were quite capable of finding trouble where it had no need to be.

The sharing did not always lead down the straight and narrow path. The two of them shared the good things and the bad. If one headed for trouble, they would both be on that path. Trouble usually came as the result of 'exploring', of which they were very fond.

While sharing a pie behind the barn, one afternoon offered other rewards. It was a perfect day for 'exploring' and the harvest crew often left things inside the barn which needed to be discovered. It was a brief search this day, as a pack of cigarettes was neatly stuffed behind one of the stairs to the barn loft. Neither had tried smoking but they had watched the men and were certain they'd be successful. It didn't appear to be that difficult. You just lit the end of the cigarette, put the other end in your mouth and breathed in. How hard could that be anyway?

Matches presented a problem and this was one thing over which Ben was watched closely. He was not allowed to play with fire. He could easily burn down the old buildings, including the house or barn. So the deed fell to the innocent Carol. Her, no one would suspect.

Gaining possession of the magic fire sticks was a success and she returned to barn in short order. The pair would now get their experiment under way.

When they found the cigarettes, they were pleased that the pack was almost full. They could smoke to their hearts' content. Smoke they did. However, before the pack was finished, they began to feel ill. Upset stomachs placed the remainder of the prize on the "tomorrow" list.

Fire often draws the interest of young children and the cousins were no exception. The glowing matches were more interesting than the lighted cigarettes. Yes, the fire drew the attention of the cousins and something had to be done with the remaining matches. Several were put inside the cigarette package and stashed carefully away for tomorrow, but they had more than would be needed.

"Let's start a fire," Ben said and found his cousin in full agreement.

They knew the straw on the barn floor would burn nicely but they also knew the barn would burn if they were going to light it on fire. They procured an old pail which sat behind the house and returned to the barn. A fire could not be started where the adults would see it. They chose to take the pail inside the barn, fill it with straw from the floor and set it ablaze.

It burned nicely. Then it flared higher and Ben panicked. He'd been warned of just this possibility and, in his panic, attempted to gain control of the blaze. He kicked the pail over on its side.

Flames nibbled away at straw on the barn floor and the pair began stomping on everything in sight. The barn would burn if they didn't act quickly. With the fire gaining momentum, they gave up their stomping and began kicking the burning straw out the barn door, onto frozen ground. Much to their relief, they managed to kick away every burning straw. The fire subsided and the barn was saved.

Both Ben and Carol decided then and there to stop smoking and never play with fire again. It had been a close call and an easy lesson this time. Next time, they may not be so lucky. No harm had been done and they hadn't been caught.

Or so they thought. Unfortunately, they had chosen the wrong bucket. Next morning when Ben's mother was in search of her bucket to scrub the house floor, she noted the remainder of the burned material and questions were posed. Ben was stumped. He swore he had no idea what had ever happened. He knew nothing about fire and reassured everyone he had not been involved and wasn't allowed to have matches.

Meanwhile, Carol was facing similar questions. She was not as strong willed as Ben and, in the face of threats of great personal harm if she didn't tell the truth, told the entire story to her mother. The jig was up and the perpetrators of the crime were caught red handed. Now punishment would ensue.

Ben felt he was the most severely punished. For Carol, it meant she could not come to visit for the next week. That was harsh for her but worse for Ben. He loved playing with his cousin and felt this was more than enough punishment for him as well. Carol's mother, however, was the baker of those wonderful lemon pies. She tossed in added punishment for Ben. There would be no more pies.

Now didn't that top it all for punishment? No Carol and no pies for a week for Ben. How could it get any worse? Yes, Ben was certain. He was being punished beyond human understanding.

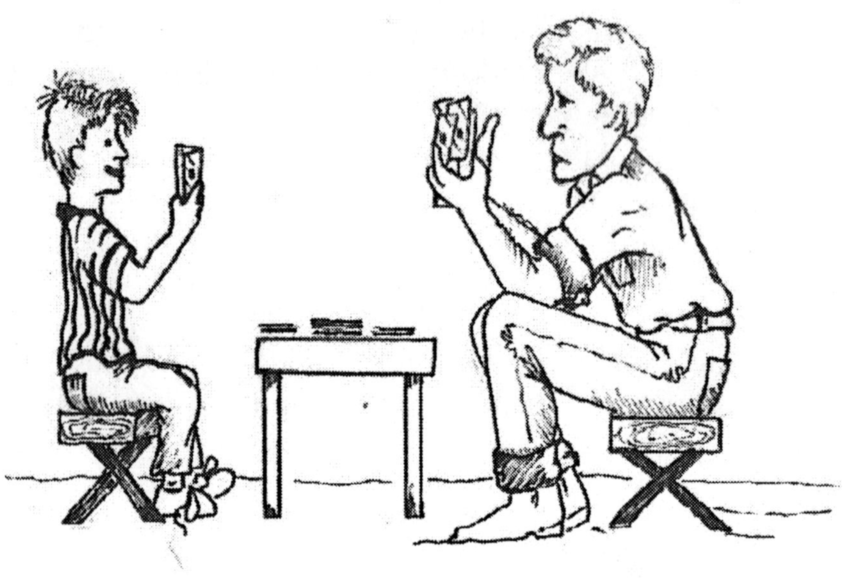

Lorriane Fee

Ben decided this one was a keeper

The Gift

Ben was excited. The ground was covered with snow, the weather remained mild and a Christmas tree sat in the little house, decorated with ornaments. Beneath it lay a few packages. It was Christmas Eve and Santa Clause was expected.

There was no chimney in the little house but he had been assured Santa would find his way in. Every year, he needed reassurance and every year the jolly old gent arrived. He had never failed in the past and he would, once again, make his appearance.

The front door opened, surprising the family and there, in the doorway, stood his sister Yvonne, a stranger by her side.

"This is Gordon," she told everyone, as the couple entered. "We're going to be married."

Ben was shocked. He liked his family just the way it was and didn't see the need for any additions. But the fellow in tow seemed pleasant enough so he decided to adopt a 'wait and see' attitude. He would scrutinize this stranger for a while and see where it would lead. His parents always cautioned him to give people a chance.

As the evening wore on, Ben decided he could learn to like the fellow his sister had brought home. He seemed to be a kind sort of fellow and now Gordon had turned his attention from the adults to him.

The unexpected happened. He was told he could open one present now! This had never happened in the past. Presents were always opened Christmas morning after Santa had come and gone. What Ben could never figure out was there were no more presents in the morning after Santa's delivery than the evening before. He knew. He had counted and recounted many times. Yet, there were always some marked from the jolly old gent in the morning and those tags were missing earlier. Besides, he could always find the cookie with the bite out of it and the half glass of milk left. No wonder Santa was chubby if he ate like that in every house.

Ben was handed a small gift and opened it. It pleased him. It was a small game with a springy strip of metal for a catapult and rings that were to be shot at a target board. "Spring Ring" it said clearly on the box. Now he would test the mettle of this newcomer.

Gordon readily agreed to the game and, with a great deal of effort, proved to be equally inept as his young competition. The games were always close, but Ben managed to win most of them. He was pleased with the outcome. Not only did this Gordon character humor him by playing silly games, but he lost more than he won.

The stranger was pretty likeable after all. Perhaps he was even worth keeping around.

All too soon, the evening drew to a close and the clock indicated midnight. He was encouraged by his family to go to bed because Santa would not come if he was awake and everyone knew Santa appeared at the stroke of midnight. Ben always wondered how he could come to so many homes at once, but the bearded old fellow always managed.

Not until twelve thirty, did Ben finally begin to climb the stairs to his bed. He had really become fond of this Gordon and it was he who had finally warned him of Santa's imminent arrival.

"You better go to bed, it's late. Santa is being delayed. He's probably been waiting outside until you're asleep so you better hurry," Gordon had told him.

That was good enough for him. If Gordon said it was true, it must be. Thus was the trust he had developed in his new friend. Yes! This one was, no doubt, a keeper.

From that Christmas on, everything changed for Ben. Gifts became more expensive and more plentiful. Spring Ring games were replaced with the most perfect holsters and cap pistols he had ever laid eyes upon or mechanical construction games and wind up toys that boggled his mind. But there were down sides too.

Upon opening a construction set, complete with bolts and wrenches, it did not impress him that he had to wait three days to play with the gift. With his brothers, Bruce and Charles, and the new brother-in-law, Gordon, working on a well drilling rig, the trio set about to construct a working model. Ben was happy to watch for the time being and amazed at the outcome of their efforts. He began to play with it. But he would sooner have constructed something himself, even if it would have been less complicated. The rig just sat on the table and whirred, pulling a piece of metal up and down on a thread. If it had wheels, maybe it could go somewhere.

As the three construction engineers turned their backs, Ben attacked. He dismantled the well drill with care and reconstructed it into... Well, he wasn't sure what it was, but he had made it. And it did have wheels to roll across the table.

Years later, Ben came to realize he had received an unexpected gift the year his sister Yvonne had first brought the stranger home. It was an intangible gift. It didn't come with a price tag and no one could buy it in a store. His two brothers were excellent role models, but now he had a third. As the years passed, he carefully watched all three of his heroes, chose what he wanted from each, put it all together, and felt he was a better person for it.

Ralph's Jitney

First it was the Great Depression and then a world war. Everything was rationed, with vital material being diverted to the war effort. The home front did with the basic necessities, while the war went on. Even the shortage of men brought change, as women were needed in production plants.

Each month, families received ration coupons which allowed them to purchase needed items. Luxury items were not included on the availability list. Foremost among those not included were cars and trucks. With production geared to the war effort, new vehicles were in demand but a shortage was experienced. Therefore, used models of transportation were refurbished or purchased from neighbors.

Here again major problems emerged. Gasoline was another rationed item. To purchase fuel for a car, one had to produce their ration tickets and these were insufficient to keep a family mobile throughout an entire month. There was one gap in the law, which was shortly discovered.

Gasoline for cars was rationed, but not for trucks. Farmers switched their mode of transportation to trucks wherever possible. When there were not enough trucks available, improvisation took over. A truck was described as a vehicle capable of hauling produce. This was the way out for the creative mind of the farmer.

Many four door sedans began to lose parts. Back seats, back doors, trunks, the back portion of roofs and even fenders seemed to disappear overnight. A little ingenuity and work and the transformation was complete as wooden boxes were added for hauling onto what had once been the family sedan. It was now a truck, and fuel was readily available.

Ralph was particular when he built his truck or 'Jitney', as they were often called. He would build the best, most attractive Jitney possible. Choosing the best wood, he struggled for days with his Jitney, using a hand saw to cut each piece to fit precisely. With the construction complete, he carefully sanded and finished the Jitney's box.

Standing back to admire his work, a feeling of accomplishment and pleasure passed over him. He had, indeed, built the best box for his Jitney ever to be seen. Throughout the neighborhood, everyone was in total agreement. Indeed, few meals were served to visiting neighbors without the topic coming up.

"Have you seen Ralph's Jitney?" someone would inevitably ask.

The reply was always the same. "Oh yes! Isn't she a beauty?"

When Ralph's wife announced that it was time for a journey to the nearest town, Ralph was overjoyed. The neighbors loved his creation. It was now time to show it off to the whole world. Perhaps as many as a hundred people would see his Jitney and comment on his work in total admiration.

Ralph beamed with pride as he steered his vehicle over the country roads, heading for town and shopping. He could already hear the comments and envision the crowd as he parked on the two block long main street. Let his wife do the shopping, he would accept praise and outline the procedure for building the perfect "truck".

Entering the streets of the town, Ralph was oblivious to his surroundings as he chatted happily with his wife, outlining his comments to the crowd which would gather. Being oblivious to the fact that he was nearing a railway crossing could have cost him his life had his wife not screamed.

"Ralph! A train!" were all the words she could get out.

Ralph looked up and sure enough a train was coming down the track, almost the same distance from the crossing as the Jitney. There was no time to stop. He would have hit the train. Ralph reacted on his only option. He floored the accelerator.

Lacking power, the Jitney did not jump forward but did pick up speed. The passengers were clear of danger and for a brief moment Ralph felt he was clear. Clear he was not. The train caught the last foot of his marvelous box and sheared it completely from the Jitney.

His creation partially destroyed, Ralph felt both relieved and cheated. He would now have to listen to "poor Ralph" comments, rather than those he had planned. But it was far from the end. The main body of what had once been a car was intact. He could always rebuild and rebuild he would. He would make the new box even more eye catching than the first.

Ralph chose the best lumber available. Taking more time for construction and finishing his new box, he stood back to view his creation. It was, indeed, better than the first.

Off to the neighbor's he went to show off his new box. He was even prouder of it than his first attempt.

"It's a beauty all right Ralph," the neighbor agreed, "even better than the first one. Don't get hit by any more trains though."

Ralph looked up, totally amused.

"Look," he said. "My Momma didn't raise no fool. That darn train took a foot off the other box so I fixed the problem. This box is one foot shorter."

And one foot shorter, it was.

Mighty White Hunters

They'd tried it all. Anything to earn a dollar was in their realm of activities. Collecting bottles lying in a ditch, trapping gophers, even hunting birds would fit the bill. But everything was seasonal and, in some cases, far too much work for the profit earned.

Collecting bottles required a great deal of walking and paid poorly for their efforts. Each weekend morning the trio would set out along a different road, towing a wagon behind. Five miles down one ditch, then five miles back in the other, usually contributed a wagon load of bottles to the cause of the young entrepreneurs. But at two cents a bottle for pop bottles and twenty cents a dozen for beer bottles, the reward was poor. Nevertheless, it would be enough to purchase needed ammunition for their twenty-two rifles later in the spring.

Next came gopher trapping. With the wildlife association paying seven cents a tail, it was a more lucrative adventure, but required even more work. Before one could snare a gopher, they had to get it out of its burrow. This required carrying buckets of water over long distances in an attempt to produce a flood. It was in this endeavor that the trio, David, Arnold and Ben, became creative. They had to consider next year's investment and, if they were to kill their prey, there would be no income for the following spring.

They neglected putting their prey to death, even though that was the expectation of those who paid the bounty. Instead, they carried a pair of very sharp scissors. One snip and the tail was theirs. With a simple maneuver, they could release their captive, barely harmed, and be ensured of an income the following spring.

With hard work required, it was somewhat frustrating when the animal in their snare had been there before and was found to be missing a vital part of their anatomy—the tail.

As spring progressed toward summer, weekend activities widened.

A more lucrative market beckoned. The wildlife association also paid a bounty on the legs of certain troublesome birds and they were readily available if one had a gun. Two of the boys did. David, however, was too young to carry a firearm legally and his duties differed. It was his responsibility to climb a tree, bother the young birds and bring the parents on the scene. The marksmen on the ground took care of the parent birds with their rifles, the young were tossed down to meet the same fate as the adults and it was on to the next cash cache.

Bullets cost one cent each and if they were successful a nest would hold four to five young birds. The catch would be seven birds at ten cents a pair for legs. They felt it was a good investment with two cents bringing forth a reward of seventy.

Other than risking his life by climbing trees fifty feet tall, David had no investment. The pair on the ground wanted to be fair and, therefore, they would make the monetary investment for the ammunition needed while their youngest friend made the effort to get the young birds. At least that's how the older boys sold the plan to poor David who received only twenty percent of the take to the elder boy's forty.

If the truth was known, both of the marksmen were deathly afraid of heights. If they had been required to climb the trees David scaled with great agility, there would have been no income whatever. David may have been aware of their fear of heights but he never let on and did his duty on a daily basis.

Jeopardy set in one sunny afternoon when David lost his footing and slipped. Twenty feet or more up a giant spruce tree in search of a nest, gravity took over. He slipped, he tumbled. Down he came through the branches. Upon hitting the ground, he proved to be healthy enough, only suffering a shortness of breath due to his brutal impact with the good earth.

Arnold and Ben checked him over quickly and concluded that no real harm had been done.

"You didn't get the young ones to call their parents," Arnold remarked to his younger brother.

"I slipped," David replied.

The excuse didn't satisfy his partners. There was work to be done to put some cash in the coffers.

"Well," Arnold said, "then get back up there and get them. We have work to do and there are other nests to find."

Poor David took one look at the tree from which he had taken the fast route down and, white face and all, made a new attempt.

The following spring David finally got his reward, got even with his older brother. While on their annual quest for gopher tails, the trio happened into a pasture with a bull.

Busily flooding out their prey, no one noticed the bull pawing the ground except David who retreated to the far side of a barbed wire fence. Suddenly, he yelled, "Look out!"

The bull was beginning his charge. Ben and Arnold dove under the bottom wire of the barbed wire fence to escape the charge, giving up their dignity and the seat of their pants on the way. David merely looked at them.

"Did you get the gopher?" he asked.

"No," Arnold replied.

Without missing a beat, David looked again at the pair lying sprawled on the ground, put his hands on his hips and said, "Then what are you waiting for? Get back in there—there is work to do you know!"

Runaway!

Little did they know the day was going to be much more eventful than they could have ever imagined. The first two wagon loads of bundles were quite routine but, as they started to return to the threshing machine with their third load, the hay rack heavily loaded, the unexpected occurred. The horses shied and bolted, frightened by some sound undetected by human ears or a sight undetected by the driver's eyes! In the batting of eye-lash, the horses were in full flight, the hay rack bouncing and rocking its way across the field.

A rabbit had leapt from behind a stock and off went the horses while the driver, Bert, pulled frantically on the reins, trying to stop the charging steeds. Pull as he would, he could not stop the runaway. The horses wouldn't even slow down. Across the field, through a little creek and up the hill they went. Just as it seemed they were about to smash into a grove of poplar trees, the horses swerved sharply to the left, throwing the loaded rack clear of its wheels. The side hit the ground and it rolled until the bundles were beneath the rack. Bert had been unceremoniously dumped in the stumble but Ben, the young rider, was under the rack and its load.

Until now, it had been a normal, rather run-of-the-mill, day. It was a break from school for the farm boy, and a pleasant way to spend it, during the time when harvest was in the fields. It was Farmers' Day, a break welcomed by children and held each fall in honor of the farmer. Of course it was meant to be a day-off and a celebration, but there was work to be done. The harvest had to come first.

A runaway team is a problem. Bert had been warned many times about his daredevil style of handling horses. He was always first to the barn at the end of the day, spurred on by hunger and a love of speed. To call him a daredevil may have been an understatement.

Speed alone was not enough for the easterner, turned threshing hand. Coming in at night always meant the horses were on the run while he stood on the front of the rack and screamed like a charging cavalry leader.

"One of these days," his lead hand warned, "you'll lose the rack and do some serious damage."

Nonetheless, Bert persisted in his ways. He was not one to be intimidated by the mere warning or the thought of danger. In fact, he thrived on it. It could never happen to him and he'd been carrying on the same way for years.

Now the accident had finally happened. The rack was on the field upside down, trapping Ben beneath it, but Bert, standing well up on the front of the rack as usual had been thrown clear. In no more time than it took to land on the ground, Bert dashed to the inverted rack, turned it on its side and began wildly throwing sheaves of grain from the great pile that covered Ben.

Trapped under the load, Ben was screaming for help, sure that each breath would be his last. Amid the bundles, there was only darkness and their weight made it impossible for him to move his arms or legs. He was certain he would never be free. But to the runaway rack driver the screaming was a pleasure, knowing that the screams were too loud for Ben to be dying and he continued to feverishly to throw the sheaves away and to fray a passage towards Ben underneath it all. Sheaves flew in all directions as Bert attempted to quiet the frightened boy below.

"Hold on Ben," he shouted, "I'm coming. I'm coming."

Hearing the shouting, other wagons appeared and began to help. Nothing needed to be said. Each wagon driver knew Bert had had a partner for the day and he was missing. There was only one place he could be, under the wagon.

An eternity passed for Ben before the last sheaf was removed. Ben took a deep breath and sat erect. Embarrassed by all the commotion he had caused there was little he could say.

"Hi Bert," was all he could manage to utter in dismay as he sat on the ground.

The pair laughed with relief and the rest of the crew, who had heard the shouting and had rushed over to help, stood with amazed looks on their faces. They were held speechless by the wagon driver and the small boy sitting amidst the bundles of grain, laughing until their sides hurt and tears streaming down their faces.

Nearby, the runaway horses grazed contentedly in the field. With a driver like Bert, it was the only rest they'd get that day.

With the wagon finally placed on its wheels and reloaded, the pair made their way to the threshing machine where Bert promised never again to be reckless.

Doubt showed on the faces of the other horsemen who knew Bert all too well. But Ben believed him. He would never break his word to him.

He didn't. Bert kept his word faithfully - right up until supper time when once again his team and wagon charged up the hill for home. Bert again perched high up on the front of the rack screaming to his heart's content.

Double Trouble

Tom and Freddie were problem children from the start. The eleventh and twelfth of the children born to the family, the pair should have been accustomed to supervision. They weren't.

The two were as close as brothers could be. They were curious, awful pranksters and their presence often put the neighbors in jeopardy.

It was difficult to tell whether disturbances around the homestead were caused by the deadly duo or an unwelcome interloper. The pair was certain to observe any unwanted guests and deal with the issue promptly. Keeping the farm safe and free from varmints was of the essence.

Once a cat happened upon the settlement and, since the family loved birds, it had to be dealt with. Tom and Freddie were dispatched to rid the birds of their threat. It also found pigeons a welcome part of its diet, as they were with the homesteading family. They would rid themselves of the pest.

However, the feline proved to be an elusive adversary. The boys attempted to catch it by hand. They did. Unfortunately, as it felt hands closing on its body, the desire for freedom became all important. It clawed its captors and escaped. Henceforth, the cat kept its distance.

Another plan was to cage the animal. To gain the upper hand, the boys would entice the cat into a cage and watch. Upon entering, a pull on a string, attached to a stick, and the gate would fall, trapping their quarry inside.

Tempting the feline into the cage required effort but eventually they were successful. Freddie pulled his string, the gate closed and Tom ran to the cage. He was too slow. The frightened animal charged toward the gate, struck it, escaped and just kept going.

It was time for drastic action. The visitor had caught and devoured several of the farm's feathered residents and must be controlled. Humane approaches were tossed aside and the pair brought gopher traps from the barn. They were set wherever the cat traveled. But they were not dealing with an average feline and most certainly not a gopher. The traps were easily avoided.

They needed a gun. Unfortunately, the family owned only a rusted antique which had passed its prime a century or so earlier. To fire the rifle, Freddie would aim at the target, holding the gun as still as humanly possible. With the trigger missing, this required Tom to strike firing pin with a hammer.

Freddie aimed at the cat, Tom struck the firing pin and the bullet struck a shed, missing the cat by ten feet. Attempt after attempt turned out the same. The cat, fearing no harm here, merely sat and looked at the pair curiously. If they wanted to make those loud noises, let them, seemed to be its attitude.

There simply had to be a better way.

Tom looked a Freddie. "Let's borrow Mr. Gerber's gun?" he suggested.

Freddie wasn't quite so sure. "Last time we borrowed his gun, we had to set the sights he said. It wouldn't hit nothin'."

"Yeah," Tom replied, "but we did sight it in."

"And that made him mad," said Freddie.

"Well, how were we to know he'd get mad? Maybe he's forgotten," Tom went on, still trying to convince his brother.

"I guess he didn't like us bouncing bullets off his barn roof 'til we could hit the weather vane," noted Freddie. "But the broad side of a barn is all the thing could hit when we started."

Further discussion ensued prior to the pair determining they'd have to try. Nothing else was working and they had been instructed to take care of the cat, regardless of what means they employed to justify their end.

Down the road they went, heading for the Gerber homestead.

Arriving at the door, the boys knocked and waited quietly. They would show Mr. Gerber their ultimate respect to make up for their earlier trespasses. He'd loaned them a rifle in the past and they needed help again. Mr. Gerber was always ready to help. But would he help them.

When Mr. Gerber answered the knock on his door and saw who it was, he was tentative. He never knew what kind of trouble this pair might bring.

"Mr. Gerber," the boys began, "sure is a nice day isn't it?"

Mr. Gerber would give them that much. The sun was shining, it was warm, yes, he had to agree; it was a nice day.

"We've kind of got a problem at home," the boys went on. There's somthin' botherin' our pigeons and we're supposed to get rid of it. We've tried everything we thought of but it didn't work. We were wonderin' if we could borrow your gun."

Their request for the firearm was granted. Mr. Gerber readily loaned the weapon, but only after warning the pair the sights were perfect and there would be no need to be bouncing any more bullets off of his barn or, even worse, shooting his weather vane to watch it twirl.

"We kinda need some bullets too," Tom told the neighbor.

Mr. Gerber complied and supplied the ammunition.

The problem would now be dispatched with ease.

Returning home, Tom and Freddie found the cat in its usual haunts as it attempted to gain access to the pigeon loft. Taking careful aim, Freddie fired. The problem had finally been taken care of.

"Job done," Freddie told his brother. "I guess we can take Mr. Gerber's stuff home."

They did. With no further use for the rifle, the boys triumphantly returned it to Mr. Gerber, along with his dead cat.

Identified Flying Objects

The Hoopers were at it again. When Grandpa and Grandma Hooper got into it, the entire neighborhood knew. They were noisy and boisterous in their disagreements.

As individuals, Grandma and Grandpa Hooper were wonderful people. Grandma Hooper had emigrated from England with her husband to set up a homestead in the new world, and now a widow, came into the marriage with twelve children. Grandpa Hooper, a widower, had also emigrated from England and brought a few children of his own into the family. They had been accepted and tended to meld together well.

The fights between the two didn't involve their children. Actually, no one, including the fighting participants really knew what started the problem. Grandpa Hooper was a quiet man but Grandma was rather feisty. When things weren't going her way, she tended to lose her temper. And when she lost her temper, things would fly.

Tonight, they were at it again. Poor Grandpa had riled his lady and she simply wasn't going to take any more. After a brief exchange of words, Grandma decided it was time to take action and get her point across to her husband.

She neared the table, picked up the sugar bowl and let it fly. A trail of sugar spread across the floor as the bowl made its way in her husband's direction. Once reaching a wall and narrowly missing its target, the glass bowl smashed to a thousand pieces against the wall.

Hearing the noise, neighbors were certain that someone would be seriously hurt. They had visited the pugilistic couple previously and nothing had come of it. They did the only thing a caring neighbor could do. They called the police but Grandpa had beaten them to it.

To a policeman, a domestic quarrel is anything but simple. It is the most unpredictable of all assignments. But they had their duty and it had to be done.

Traveling to the Hooper farm, two officers approached the front door with extreme caution. They had never been called out that way before but had heard about the Hoopers and their activities. This was something they would rather not be involved in. The officers knocked on the door and waited.

Shortly, it was opened by the diminutive Grandma Hooper.

"Good evening Mrs. Hooper," the senior officer greeted the lady of the house. "Is there a problem?"

"There's no problem at all," Grandma Hooper responded.

"But," said the officer, "your neighbors and Mr. Hooper called us that there was a disturbance."

"That man would disturb anyone," Grandma replied.

"Well," the officer continued, "The neighbors told us you were throwing things at Mr. Hooper."

"No I wasn't," said Grandma petulantly.

"Now Mrs. Hooper," the officer insisted, "Did you throw a sugar bowl at your husband?

"I did not," Grandma Hooper said, denying the entire incident.

"But, madam," said the officer. "We were told you threw a sugar bowl."

"Yes," Grandma admitted at last, "I threw a sugar bowl."

"Then you admit it," responded the policeman.

"I don't admit anything," Grandma Hooper replied. "I threw a sugar bowl. But not at him."

For a moment, a confused look passed over the officer's face.

"No Sir!" said Grandma. "If I'd have thrown it at him, I'd have hit him!"

Lorriane Fee

Ryan loved Christmas and wheels

Mini Mechanic

Bruce was a mechanic. In fact, he was one of the best of his era. He could listen to a machine and know exactly what the problem was, even without electronic equipment.

Therefore, it was natural that his son, Ryan, would also be a mechanic. He was always there when his father repaired the family car, even though he was somewhat confused by the issue. To Ryan, the car was running perfectly. It managed to get the family to A&W for chicken and always brought them home. So why was his father taking the car apart?

As he attempted to come up with an answer, Ryan's confusion passed. He became amused. His father must be taking things apart to see how they worked. He noticed. that the car was always put back together again. This must be what a mechanic did. Being a curious boy, he determined that he could do anything his father could, although on a smaller scale as he was only five years old. He couldn't work on the big machines with those big wrenches but he could definitely repair his toy cars.

His career began early. Unlike many children, he discovered what he wanted to be when he grew up at a very young age. He would be a mechanic! He knew he'd love the job because he loved to take things apart, just like his Dad did.

Ryan went to his toy box and took out several toy cars. Lining them up in a row so each imaginary customer would be served in order, he began his work. It seemed each car had a wheel problem, because they were the first to be disassembled. Then there were the axels, the doors and anything else that could possibly be taken off. It became a father-and-son activity. Ryan disassembled each unit and his father would put them back together. This led to no end of amusement on the part of the boy and father and son togetherness.

Of the entire year, Ryan enjoyed Christmas the most. This is not unusual, as many children look forward with great anticipation to the arrival of dear old Santa Claus. But to Ryan, it was different. It was the one time of year that he would see several toys, all in need of being broken down into their basic parts. It was hard work, but he would get the job done, even if it took all Christmas Day. He was dedicated to his purpose.

Of course, his father could spend all Boxing Day putting the toys back together. Eventually, Bruce didn't even bother. He had bought his son several construction sets but this was not Ryan's forte. He didn't want to construct anything. He wanted to take it apart and see how it worked.

Time passed, toy cars were of little interest. They had only a few moving parts, wheels. Once they were lying in a heap on the living room floor, the toy held little interest. He needed a greater challenge.

There it was, sitting right on his parent's night table. A wind up alarm clock sat and stared at him as it ticked away, marking the seconds. This would be a challenge!

Undaunted by the awesome task, the boy escaped with the clock and disappeared into his room. He could do this and there was no need to worry, his father would put it together when he came home from work.

Ryan proved to be very skillful at his work. In no time at all, he had the complete clock disassembled. Unfortunately for his parents, his father could not manage to put it together and was late for work the next day.

From that day on, the family had a problem. They could not keep alarm clocks in the house. Regardless of where they put them, Ryan would find them and reduce them to pieces. Until he grew somewhat older, clocks would suffice.

OK fine! Maybe he wouldn't be a mechanic, his parents thought. Maybe he'll be a jeweler. At least he's good at working with his hands.

The never content Ryan eventually became bored with the challenge offered by clocks and moved on. Fine! Scratch the jeweler too.

For Christmas, he was given a new camera. Somewhat older, he needed a new challenge and, perhaps, he would enjoy photography. He did. At least, he did for a while.

But the camera began to act in a strange manner. He had to repair it.

Predictable as it may be, he took the camera apart only to discover he could not reassemble the one hundred odd pieces it had required to construct it. He turned to his father. This time, Bruce was of little help.

With his Uncle Gordon visiting Ryan had an idea. Uncle Gordon could make anything and fix anything. Out he came with a cardboard box containing the camera in its many pieces.

"Uncle, can you fix this?" he asked.

His uncle took one look, laughed and said, "I think this one is history."

Yes, Ryan was a master at disassembling anything. But his talent would only have been of value had he a job in recycling.

For some reason, he never did learn how to put things back together.

Pregnant Idea

Freddie was up early. There were chores to complete and a visit to the neighbor's house was in order. He had given his word that today he would be there early to help. The neighbor needed meat to feed his family and this time it would consist of a large sow which had to be butchered, cut and prepared for the table.

Although a difficult job, it was anything but unusual for Freddie to help his neighbors, especially with butchering livestock. He was considered the best at this sort of tasks and quite a few others, in the farming community. He did all his own work and helped neighbors willingly and often. They thanked him and showed their momentary appreciation but rarely returned the favor. In spite of this, Freddie continued to be the community helper whenever he was asked.

Hurrying somewhat with his morning chores, he fed the livestock, milked cows and separated the milk into skim milk and cream. With the cream in its cans ready for shipping, he managed time for a quick breakfast before trekking to the neighboring farm, down the road.

It would be a relatively easy job this time. The neighbor, James Crawford, had promised to have everything ready for the slaughter. This meant a tripod with ropes to raise the pig, a barrel filled with boiling water in which to dip the pig to make removing the bristly hair simpler and an area for cutting the meat into useable sizes. They needed bacon, roasts, ham and an entire assortment of meat to use for the making of sausages. The excess fat would be boiled later and, with the addition of lye, made into laundry soap. The morning should be enough time, after which he would return home to his own duties.

Breakfast and chores completed, Freddie set off down the lane, along a short piece of road and up the Crawford lane to get to the work which awaited him. He sang to himself as walked along, thoroughly content with his life and even the work before him. Helping the neighbors was a joy in itself.

As he topped the small rise in the Crawford lane, he was puzzled. There was no tripod, no ropes and no barrel of boiling water to be seen. Had the Crawford's forgotten what was to happen on this day? It would take a great deal more time to finish the job now that nothing was prepared. He set about finding firewood and a boiling barrel in the yard, alone with his work. He'd simply have to get things ready himself. Content with his fire and the barrel filled with water, he located a tripod and some ropes and began to set them in place. Still, Mr. Crawford had not appeared. Perhaps the family was ill. If so he'd either do the entire job alone or wait for another day.

Still bewildered, Freddie knocked on the Crawford door.

Mr. Crawford answered momentarily. "Oh, hello Freddie he said. C'mon in and have a coffee."

Freddie entered but wondered why the work was being put off.

"What's the problem," he asked. "You were to have everything ready so we could get the butchering done?"

Through his mind, Freddie passed the thought that, being new to farming and the community, Mr. Crawford had not known how to prepare for a butchering. Perhaps he had misunderstood his instructions and was puzzled with it all. Freddie resigned himself to this new set of circumstances and prepared his mind for more work and the deliverance of a lesson on butchering procedure.

"Why didn't you have everything ready?" Freddie queried... and went on. "It doesn't matter, it's all ready now. We'll get at it as soon as I finish my coffee."

"Well, Freddie," Mr. Crawford began, "there's a bit of a problem come up. I think you better come on down to the pig pen with me. We gotta look at somethin'."

Another delay was obvious and Freddie readied himself for spending the entire day helping the neighbor rather than getting his own work done. It was fall, a busy season for every farmer and he was doing a neighborly favor, not offering to spend his entire day away from home.

Making their way toward the pig pens the pair found light conversation was the mode of the day. The weather, would we get the crops in... and anything else that had absolutely no relevance until the demise of a pig was brought up. The pig topic was never broached until the farmers reached the pig pens.

"You know, Freddie," said Mr. Crawford. "The doggonedest thing happened. I went out to light the fire, boil the water, put up the ol' tripod and get everything done you told me about, but thet sow din't cooperate. No sir! She din't cooperate one bit."

"Have a look in there," he said motioning to the pig pens.

When Freddie peered into the pig pen, there lay a very contented mother pig with several young piglets nursing quietly.

"Yessir!" Mr. Crawford went on. "I never would have believed it but I guess she didn't want to be dinner. This mornin' that darn ol' pig gave birth to a whole litter of healthy lil' ones. Seems she'd sooner be a mother than food."

Freddie made his way home to relay the story to his family. But he had to wonder how anyone would make a successful farmer if they couldn't tell when an animal was pregnant.

In The Clover

She was one mean lady. Regardless of where you wanted to chase her, whip or no whip, she simply refused to follow orders.

She was a man hater. When trying to chase her into a pen, she would put her head down and charge. And of all men, she hated John the most. Moving her from pen to pen, when John attempted to turn her and head her in another direction, she would lower her head, horns and all, run over the man and more often than not, break his glasses, leaving him and the glasses lying on the road.

He had had enough. It was time to ship the cow, which caused him grief. It would have happened long ago except for one minor detail. Her calves were always strong and healthy. Fortunately, the calves did not have their mother's attitude toward men or the human race. They were docile and friendly.

Yet, the day came to load the four footed lady on to a truck and take her to auction. Again, she was proving to be less than cooperative. John, his son-in-law, and two friends were attempting to direct her into a livestock chute and a truck. In spite of their efforts, she turned short of the loading chute on every occasion and headed back into the corral.

"If she goes in the truck, we'll drop the gate fast," John told his helpers. "Chase her in and I'll get the gate."

The plan seemed sound. No headway was being made with four herders in the corral so three would do. John was left to close the gate on the truck, trapping his nemesis within the box.

By moving forward, one man on each side of the cow, and one behind, the lady trotted in the right direction, at last. The cow was moving toward the chute and her head was within inches of the narrow opening. To ensure success, Ben slapped the old girl on the flank. It worked. She headed up the incline on a run and into the truck box.

John jumped down to close the opening to impede the cow's departure. Unfortunately, the cow was faster. She entered the box, turned and headed for the opening where the gate was supposed to be. John found himself in jeopardy.

As his feet touched the floor of the livestock chute, the cow was there, her head down and charging. He was knocked down, run over and another pair of glasses needed replacing. This was one lady who had no intention of taking a truck ride, going to market or finding a new owner.

The effort began again.

Again the cow headed into the chute. Again she was hit on the flank but this time with a small stick. She moved forward.

She became excited and let nature take its course just as the stick was coming forward. A splatter came from the cow and caught Ben and his partner in the face and mouth. It was beyond imagination. This was something they would never choose to eat.

To their surprise, it was not as distasteful as they would have imagined.

Wiping his face, Ben smiled and looked at his partner.

"What do you think" he asked.

His partner spat the cow droppings from his mouth and replied, "Clover."

This time, John was quicker on the gate. The cow was loaded and off to auction. But she had her say before her departure.

Lorriane Fee

Now where did that come from?

The Big Shot

Ben never left home. In actual fact, his home left him as his father went to work on the drilling rigs and his mother moved twenty miles away to become a housekeeper for a small town doctor. Ben was alone in a basement apartment to fend for himself.

Worst of all, no one had taught him to cook. He did the best he could to make a meal and fill his stomach with whatever was available. Usually, it was potato chips, which had no nutritional value but, at least, took away the pangs of hunger.

His parents returned on weekends – an 'event' to which Ben looked forward each every week-day. He was sixteen years old and not equipped to make a life for himself. Nevertheless, he did manage to keep busy whenever he wasn't skipping school.

How well he remembered his father's last warning before he left for work and left the boy alone.

"Be careful with guns and never let anyone else near them," he had said.

Ben was always careful with guns and loved to hunt. It was the second part of the warning that caused him the problem. His best friend, Arnie, also loved to hunt but had no shotgun. Ben found two in the house, one semi automatic twelve gauge belonging to his brother, and the second a double barrel, which he preferred.

Day after day, just to keep themselves busy, the boys went walking through pasture and wood, caring not what they came across but being free, spending time - each carrying a gun. On occasion, there was the opportunity to blast away at something, but tin cans were the most common targets.

The day came when Arnie wanted to go hunting with another friend who came un-armed - he needed a gun. It took pleading on Arnie's part, but Ben agreed to lend him his brother's rifle, with the caution that he must be careful, return it in good condition and never tell a soul. Arnie was jubilant.

When the gun was returned, Ben was not certain his instructions had been followed. He placed the butt of the gun on the floor and pulled back the action to ensure it was unloaded before placing it back in storage. No one would ever know he had disobeyed.

Inspecting the action for live ammunition, his finger slipped. The action moved forward and an ear shattering blast came from the barrel. The muzzle was so close to his head, Ben felt the heat from the pellets. Nor did the blast prove to be harmless. A very neat circle appeared in the ceiling of the basement apartment and a shouting landlady appeared at his door.

"What happened?" she demanded. "There's a hole in my hardwood floor in the living room and marks on the ceiling. And the hole is right where my niece had been sitting only a minute ago, and my carpet is ruined."

Ben did his utmost to explain the situation, without admitting the truth.

On the weekend, his parents arrived home and the situation was still unresolved. His father wanted an explanation and the boy did his best to supply one.

"There was a hotplate on the floor and I was cooking some pork chops," he said. "I dropped a shotgun shell on it and it exploded and went right up through the ceiling."

His father did not question the explanation for a moment. Ben felt a breath of fresh air, with some assurance that his Dad had believed him. He was off the hook.

However, his brother soon asked if he would like to go to an uncle's farm for the weekend. Always up for a trip to the farm, the younger brother agreed.

The weekend was wonderful, but Ben knew he had to return home and, on doing so, he had decided to tell the entire truth regarding the hole in the ceiling. He had not been brought up to lie and avoiding the truth was bothering him.

He had little chance to go into details before he was confronted by his father.

"Could you tell me one more time what happened here?" the older man asked.

"Well Dad," Ben began, "I know I wasn't supposed to but I loaned out the shotgun. When I got it back, I was checking to make sure it wasn't loaded when it went off and blew a hole through the ceiling."

"Make's sense to me," said Ben's father, calmly pulling the gun and a broomstick from behind his back.

The older man set the butt of the gun on the floor, right under the hole, stuck one end of the broomstick through the hole and the other end on the muzzle of the gun.

"Neat isn't it?" said the boy's father.

He had known all along and was happy his son was safe and allowed time on the farm for Ben to build up the courage to admit his mistake. He had actually asked the older brother to take Ben there to allow him time to consider the situation.

The landlady's floor was repaired and Ben never again loaned out any guns.

In the end, it was an excellent lesson for the boy, taught by the best teacher of them all, experience and a parent, although he wondered how his father had known the truth.

Could it be he'd had a similar experience?

Blessed be the Mouth

If Marv had only one gift in life, it would be his mouth. It wasn't so much what he said but how and when he said it. With his innocent, child-like face, everyone had to believe him, even his lies. And he was, indeed, capable of lies.

Traveling with Ben, the younger Marv set the scene and Ben merely followed the lead by attempting to make what his partner said sound ridiculous. Time after time, Ben would attempt to quiet his young friend as he expounded on his favorite subject, the sixty four MGB, which the pair used for travel.

It was true that to travel the pair had to pick up odd jobs, being paid cash only, and would work at anything. If both could find work for a week, they could travel for two months without worry. The main expense was always gas for the car.

On occasion, living did prove a bit simple. Home made Ketchup soup or a visit to a smorg where they would fill their pockets with food before leaving was not unusual. But only once did they have to resort to theft. That time it had been a block of cheese and box of crackers from a grocery store, even then they nearly got caught.

Accommodations normally found them in the great outdoors, sleeping on the ground. Only in the rain, did they search for shelter. That was often the local police station where they were allowed to sign in and sleep in a cell over night without charges being laid.

For the creative duo, there was yet one more way to make cash. That was to take advantage of the local rubes. For this, they needed smaller towns, a restaurant or drive-in and a bunch of guys talking about their 'hot' cars. Inevitably, Marv would go into action with Ben in his supportive role.

"Heck!" Marv would say. "Your big engines aren't so much. We've got a four banger outside that does wheelies."

This of course referred to the fact that the MGB had only a four cylinder engine. No fan of the American monster would ever believe such a line.

Ben would interject, "C'mon Marv. Knock it off; we don't need to hear this."

But Marv would continue, often moving to sit with the marks and carry on.

Ben, on the other hand, remained at his table furiously attempting to quiet his friend who became more and more exuberant as the moments passed.

With his goal reached, one of the local hot rodders insisting he was a liar, he finished the act.

"Tell you what," he'd say. "I've got twenty bucks. Wanna match it? We'll put a stone on the road with the twenties underneath. If the wheels come up, the money's ours. If they don't it's yours."

The hook, bait and sinker had been swallowed. This, the locals had to see, and adding a twenty to their pockets would be icing on the cake.

Acting as frustrated as one could be, Ben would agree to Marv's antics and the rubes would have lighter pockets as the front wheels did, indeed, rise and the visitors scooped up their money. All that was left was the disappearance of tail lights over the first hill and a happy pair of travelers.

They knew there was always the possibility of losing their last twenty but it had never happened and they were certain of success. Only once, did Ben question his partner when the act began.

Having the challenge accepted, he mentioned to Marv that they didn't have twenty dollars.

"Got a buck?" was all Marv said.

"C'mon," Ben replied. "That'll fool them in the dark, but what if the wheels come down or don't go up?"

"Never happened before," said the optimistic Marv.

Although crazy, the ruse was on. Money placed under a rock, Ben revved the car's engine and pushed in the clutch. But his foot slipped. The wheels didn't rise.

Without a moment of hesitation, Marv reached out an open door, scooped up the cash and yelled, "Hit it!"

Hit it Ben did. The car jumped forward and this time the tail lights disappeared into the night much faster than usual with the driver looking in the rear view mirror as much as he was at the road.

It was Ben who finally lost his control. Pulling up in front of a restaurant, he found the local drag champion to be less than humorous.

"What's that thing?" he asked as he stared at the small sports car. "Does it have a motor or do you push pedals?

Ben didn't like the attitude or comments. Today, he may own not one but two cars and suggested a race up a seven mile mountain road with its curves and switch backs.

"Why don't we see?" he said. "Let's race for pinks up the seven miles and back.

First one back, get's both cars."

The challenge was readily accepted.

Ben knew he could get a lead at the start, but also knew he'd be passed going up the hill. He was counting on the MG's maneuverability and handling to make a quick u-turn at the top and head into those curves on the way down.

As expected, he was passed but had held on longer than expected. He came to the top of the hill on the rear bumper of a rather fast hot rod. One crank of the wheel and he was turned and headed downhill, gaining an advantage as the larger car looked for a suitable place to turn. The curves added to his lead and a jubilant MG driver arrived in front of the restaurant much to the surprise of onlookers who were certain their buddy would own a nice sports car.

The hot rodder appeared minutes later and, true to his word, handed over his registration.

"You know," Ben told him, "I never did like big cars. You can have it back if you go into that restaurant, stand on a table and in a very loud voice announce to everyone that the MG is the greatest automobile ever made. Say it three times then crow like a rooster."

It was humiliation at its very best. But a man needs his car. As the rooster crowed, Ben handed over the registration slip and chuckled his way out the door and into the night.

Nuts!

Nuts! That's what they were. There was no doubt about it. The scheme was nuts. The plan was nuts. They were simply nuts to even consider it.

But then, to the boys, way back in '58, a hundred bucks was a lot of money. And it seemed the get-rich scheme could work if they only had another pair of accomplices. Ben and Arnold set out to find these as soon as possible and it proved to be an easy feat. Bobby and Jock signed on to the plan immediately, hoping to gain their share of the ill-gotten gains. For their part, they were promised twenty dollars for two minutes' work, not including practice. Of course, they had no idea the actual reward was much higher or they may not have been quite so agreeable.

Practice they did. Day after day, hour after hour, they practiced. This would have to be perfect. Armed with the needed tools, each of the four villains attacked their job, ready to ensure the feat would go off without difficulty. Five minutes, four minutes, the times were growing shorter, but it wasn't enough. Ben and Arnold insisted the foursome must be finished within two minutes to ensure a smooth getaway from the crime scene.

At last, the gang had dropped their time to under two minutes.

"That's good," Ben told his crew. "It will take a little longer doing the real thing. We have no idea how tight they'll be but I think we've learned the tricks. Now we have some watching to do."

For a full week, the gang met, just after dark and journeyed to the town's main street. Timing was important. Their subject had to be as regular as clockwork in his habits. He was. His arrival at the coffee shop was within a five minute period for the entire seven days. They were ready.

On the chosen night, Bobby, the only one with a driver's license, arranged to borrow his father's car, a Volkswagen beetle which would be easy to maneuver.

Climbing in, the perpetrators headed for Main Street and the coffee shop, planning to arrive shortly after dark. It was fall and darkness came early which was much to the liking of the devastating crew. They parked. They waited and they watched.

At the predicted time, the car arrived and parked in front of the coffee shop. Its occupants emerged and then disappeared within the establishment – so far, so good. Everything was going strictly according to plan. Breathing from the four gangsters quickened as the hour of their crime approached. They had nothing against the car driver, but Ben's brother did, and he had offered the monstrous reward.

Taking their tools in hand, the boys quietly moved from their car to the waiting vehicle. There on its side, in large lettering, was the word Police. Why they were told to carry out their dastardly deed on the commanding officer of the local police force, they had no idea. They only knew if they wanted their hundred bucks, they had to choose the right car. This was it.

Their feat was planned well; each boy advanced on the car and approached a designated tire. The lack of hubcaps would make their chore so much easier. Further simplicity was offered as no car jacks were needed. The deed could be accomplished with the car sitting quietly on its wheels.

With star wheel wrenches in hand, they knelt to their jobs. Within the two minute time-frame, Ben insisted upon, they were to be done.

The first turn of a lug nut gave an ominous squeaking sound that sent chills up the villains' spines. However, a quick glance around showed no one on the street and the police chief and his partner could be seen through the café window, still enjoying their coffee and chatting-up the waitress. The procedure continued.

Seconds became hours in their minds, but the chore was complete. The police car sat in its place, firmly on its tires. But the lug nuts were in the pockets of four boys.

"Let's do it," Ben said.

Loading into their car, they backed quietly from the curb.

"Hit it!" Ben commanded the driver.

Tires screamed on the pavement and the car jumped forward. But there was no response from within the café.

Indeed, it took several passes of screaming rubber before the objects of the night's efforts emerged into the darkened street. With burning rubber right in front of them, daring them to react, the police had only one course of action. They jumped into the police car, slammed it into gear and backed away from the curb.

"Got a problem," Arnold noted. "The wheels are staying on that thing. Let's get out of here."

But as the officer behind the wheel turned the steering wheel and gunned the motor of the police cruiser to give chase, the plan showed perfection. The two front wheels simply fell to the pavement, one back wheel fell beneath the car, the second rolled down the street and a shower of sparks lit up the night as brake drums spun on the pavement. The deed was done.

Laughter broke the night air, drowning out the profanities from the direction of the police car.

"C'mon," said Ben. "We got 'em. Let's go get our money."

Porter Panic

For the young traveler, the whole idea seemed exciting. It was his first time on an airplane and he was heading for Chicago.

By modern standards, the flight would have meant little as air travel became popular and an everyday occurrence. But this flight was the farm boy's first and he didn't mind that it would be long. Modern jets travel the distance in practically no time at all. This was before their time and the passenger was to take their flight aboard a propeller driven plane. It was a lengthy trip but would allow time to peer down at the terrain passing below.

Passing through the airport and boarding the plane, the farm boy looked around him. There were many passengers boarding the same flight. This, in itself, was amazing to a youth who was not well traveled and had often stood in amazement at the number of passengers who would climb on a bus or a single railway car.

Lifting off the tarmac, a slight shiver passed over his body. Would this plane make the trip? Would it ever come to earth again without crashing? There were just too many safety questions so he, eventually, put his fears aside and rested in his seat. Little did he realize the height the plane would achieve before taking a tentative look out through a window. There below him, farms seemed to spread out forever, a patchwork quilt on the landscape. *This plane better land,* he thought, *or it's going to be one big bump when we hit the ground.* He wondered if they issued parachutes to passengers should the plane experience difficulties. Assuring himself they would, he once again settled back for a nap.

Hours passed, shortened by his frequent naps before the pilot finally announced they were approaching their destination. He readied himself for the bump ahead and watched out the window as the earth came closer. It was coming closer at an amazing rate and he had been warned to wear a seat belt, "just in case." He didn't like the situation one bit. He closed his eyes and waited.

With a slight screeching sound from the tires and a very slight bump, less than he had experienced while riding in the family car on country roads, the aircraft settled down on the runway and taxied to a complete stop. Mobile staircases appeared out of nowhere and the passengers disembarked.

Once again, the terminal was crowded. He had never seen as many people milling around in the small town mall the family used when shopping for necessities. Some were waiting, others boarding planes, some buying tickets and yet others disembarking or looking for their baggage.

He had no idea where he would find his suitcase. He had left it on a cart before boarding and hoped it had arrived with him. But it could have been left in the airport of departure.

A friend was to meet him and, much to his pleasure, he began to relax when he noticed the friendly face.

"C'mon over here," the friend said. "We'll get your bags."

As promised, the bags appeared down a chute as if by magic.

It was a comforting feeling to meet up with a friend who understood the workings of this complicated way of life. He knew his friend was experienced by now. He'd flown into Chicago a full week earlier.

The farm boy picked up his bag and began to make his way to the door, his friend leading the way. Passing through it, he was accosted.

"Could I carry yer bayag sir," an elderly porter asked.

Looking at the porter, an elderly African American gentleman, the first reaction was one of amazement. Only once had he seen such a gentleman before, and that was on a threshing crew when he was still a boy. He had admired his first encounter with a man of this type and felt a kinship instantly but did not need help with his bag.

"No thank you," he replied.

A few steps later, he noticed the porter was following him.

"But Ahd like to carry yer bayags sir," he repeated.

Once again came the same reply. "No thank you, I can carry them."

A short distance later, the porter once again made the request.

"But sir! Could ah please carry yer bayags?"

Somewhat distressed by the porter's persistence, the farm boy's city cousin attempted to take the situation into his own hands. He made both the decision to back his friend and to end the harassment.

"It's alright," he said, "they aren't heavy."

The elderly gentleman looked the newcomer to the conversation straight in the eye and, without blinking, had one comment.

"An' jest how'd you know," he said. "You ain't carryin 'em?"

The gentleman had made his point and was handed the small bag.

Smiling contentedly, he made his way along with the travelers to a waiting taxi cab, opened the trunk and gently placed the bag inside before closing the lid.

Waiting patiently for eye contact the porter stood like a statue. On recognition, he smiled again, looked at his traveler, held out his hand and said, "Jest anything you'd like sir!"

The tip was little pay for the experience.

Bee Line

While in university, students face the financial challenges of tuition, books and simply living. For Tim, as with many others, this meant summer jobs, which were not always of one's choosing. A job is a job and Tim had to take whatever he could find, for the coming summer, he was scraping the bottom of barrel. Jobs were tight, so it was off to obtain a professional driver's license and sit behind the wheel of a taxi in the hot summer sun. It was all he could find and it would have to do.

Much to his surprise, the license proved quite accessible. In spite of giving him the legal right to drive semi-trailers or any other vehicle on wheels, he found it unnecessary to rent or borrow a truck for the driving portion of the test. A Chevy station wagon would do just fine, he was told.

A station wagon it was as he went through all the maneuvers necessary and jumped through the hoops to gain the needed license. And his examiner was a man who obviously liked hoops. Turn right, turn left, straight ahead, through a school zone, by a construction site and anything else that popped into his head, which may fail a student, seemed to be his calling.

Passing the driving test with flying colors, Tim was now off to the taxi office, license in hand to solidify his hold on a job. This too, proved to be no challenge. After two days as a student driver, with an experienced hand as an overseer, he was directed to his own unit. He was on the road!

Or was he? He was told there was one more requirement. He had a driver's license and a job 'if'... He didn't like that 'if'. He required a city permit to operate a cab. No test was needed, just a criminal record check, a driving record check and an interview.

That driving record check bothered him. Tim had a tendency to speed and had recently picked up a few citations. As expected, his past had caught up to him and the interview proved lengthy. Questions were answered respectfully and, after promising to never, never speed again, the interviewer granted his permit with a warning.

"One more ticket," he said, "and it's good-bye permit."

The idea bothered Tim although losing the permit was not problematical. One more ticket and he'd lose his driver's license anyway.

From that point on, through the summer's heat, he would no longer be Tim. No siree, Bob. From now on, he was cab number 83.

He found that the radio dispatcher liked numbers better than any other words. When one is dealing with numbered addresses throughout a twelve hour shift, this was to be expected. Every communication between dispatcher and driver involved numbers, either as destinations or codes. Codes limited air time for the busy company radio and made communication clear and concise.

Tim learned all his codes, warned that a code Red should always be followed by his location. This meant he was in trouble and would bring cabbies flying from all directions to assist him with his problems and prompt a call to the police. Wondering if he would actually receive help, he had to try that code. It worked. The action was fast and furious and taxis and police cruisers converged on him. His decision led to a pop in the nose, an interview with both the police and his manager, but he still had a job.

His favorite codes were two, three and six. Two and three were designed to let the dispatcher know how long he would be away from his cab and radio with two meaning coffee and three meaning lunch. Yet his very favorite was code six. It meant he could turn in his cab, head home and forget the day's frustrations.

That is not to say there weren't some amusing and exciting times during the summer. On one occasion, Tim pulled into a taxi zone in front of one of the city's sleaziest hotels to encounter a highly intoxicated, middle aged man.

Crawling into the cab and giving his address proved to be a problem. But that was merely the tip of the iceberg. Soon, Tim's passenger was shouting at him to "pass, change lanes, hurry," or any other instruction that happened to cross his soggy mind. Tim took it all in stride. He'd been through this before and had come to expect anything. But when the passenger reached across the front seat, swore and grabbed the cab's steering wheel, he had gone too far. The situation was getting dangerous.

Tim did what any experienced cabby would have done. He smacked his passenger right in the mouth and threatened him with a trip to the police station, a trip which would prove unnecessary. His passenger sat back, folded his arms and smiled the rest of the way home.

Reaching his destination, new problems arose. With the foggy brained passenger safely poured out of the cab, Tim couldn't believe his ears.

"I have to go in the house for some money," blurted the waddling passenger as he slammed the cab's rear door shut. "I spent everything at the bar. I'll be right back," he yelled almost falling over the front yard gate.

"That's it," Tim thought as he saw his passenger disappear around a corner. "I'm stiffed and it's a pretty big fare."

True to his word, foggy brain reappeared, paid his fare and tipped and Tim twenty bucks.

"Not bad!" said Tim to himself. "I'll have to smack a few more passengers if it gets me tips like this."

From that day forward, as the days rolled on, Tim would find, what was soon to become his favorite passenger, leaning against the hotel wall and awaiting his arrival. Of course other cabbies, ahead of him in line, always got excited. The rule was first in, first out at the cab stands.

But good old "soggy brain" as he came to be known, would look at them in disgust, and announce, "I'm goin' with my lil' buddy. He knows how to hannel me."

Each time, the scene was replayed, including the twenty dollar tip.

However, not all was honey and sunshine for the new cabbie. He was prone to let his sense of humor get in the way from time to time.

Called in to have his cab serviced, he sat in the car atop the garage hoist singing, "Please 'regrease' me let me go." This found him left sitting on a hoist, six feet in the air, for four hours and wondering how to get down since nature seemed to be calling.

Arriving at work one morning he was told to park in front of a hotel, the York. The problem was, the dispatcher had a distinct accent and lacked any form of a sense of humor. Therefore, he instructed Tim to "Paak at de Yoik."

After an hour's wait, the dispatcher came on the air.

"I wonder where eighty 'tree' might be?" Tim heard him say.

Without thinking, Tim replied, "Paaked at de Yoik."

He was promptly sent back to the garage with the instruction to go home. It looked like it was going to be a short day.

The cabby supervisor had a different opinion. "Forget it and get on the road," he was told.

Tim picked up his mike, gave the radio his cab number and waited.

"Yeah, eighty three," replied the dispatcher.

"Hi there! I'm back," Tim told him.

For the rest of the day, he hauled nothing but elderly ladies with bags of groceries from any store the dispatcher could find. To Tim, it was a surprise to see just how many stores there were in the city and how many elderly ladies expected him to carry their groceries.

All good things, and bad ones, must come to an end, and for Tim, this meant being relieved of his job. While traveling down a main thoroughfare with a dignified lady in the back seat, an unwanted visitor made its appearance through the cab window. A large bee had decided to hitch a ride and, although Tim wasn't afraid of much, bees and snakes were where he drew the line.

Hitting the brakes, he brought the cab to a speed where he could bail out. And bail he did. Unfortunately, when he stopped the cab didn't. It jumped a curb, found its way down an incline and came to a rest against a tree. Neither his passenger nor the cab company found this experience satisfactory even though it did prove exciting.

The passenger wrote a letter to the cab company. The cab company supervisor wrote a letter to Tim. And Tim went home. This time to stay.

Lorriane Fee

Bob was pleased with his surprise drink

Fingering It Out

They were the new kids on the block. Working at their first job and fresh out of high school, there was a great deal for the pair to learn about office life and the company for which they worked. Toss in the fact that they were total greenhorns at life, especially in the city, and had few developed social skills and they were simply fish out of water.

With less than a month to grow used to the office environment, Bob and Ben found themselves shipped off, some two hundred miles north, with a group of experienced workers. New company products were in the offing, ready to be introduced in the near future and three weeks of study was needed. For the experienced workers on the sales crew, this would be run of the mill. They'd seen it all before and had a firm foundation upon which to further their skills. But for the rookies, it was a major assignment. They were still unfamiliar with the old products and now they needed to begin their training with new ones and nothing to build on.

So off to head office they went, over ice covered winter roads which added to Ben's fears. He knew the driver of their car was speeding and paying no attention whatever to road conditions. The vehicle would tend to slip from time to time on the ice covered road but the driver seemed oblivious to the fact. Several times, both Ben and Bob had hinted that slowing down would be a great idea—to no avail.

An hour into the drive, they watched across the highway as a car skidded out of control and struck a tow truck, already trying to unscramble an accident. The point was finally made, and at last the driving resumed at a much slower pace—to the passengers' relief.

Further shocks awaited the pair. They were traveling north and the temperature seemed to drop steadily with each mile. By the end of the trip, it had dipped to minus forty and along with the wind, chilled the southerners to the bone. They were neither dressed nor prepared for such a cold welcome. Even the old car's heater couldn't seem to keep pace with the dropping thermometer.

The crew entered the lobby of an old, but elegant hotel. Procuring their room keys, Bob and Ben found they were to be room-mates. Perhaps they could reassure each other and make it through this ordeal with at least limited success.

With dinner that evening, they were followers. They followed the debonair leaders of the group, watched carefully and mirrored their moves. It didn't seem difficult, although they were in a restaurant far more formal than any they had seen before. Success adds to success and confidence, and as the dinner progressed, the pair of rubes began to relax. The dinner went well.

With a certain degree of self-assurance setting in, the pair decided they would dine alone the following evening. They had been apprentices the night before and now felt they could unfold their wings and fly with the best. They would be suave and debonair.

They chose an eatery which offered a wide variety of dishes but were somewhat taken aback by the greeting they received at the door. A suited gentleman in white gloves asked if they had reservations. Of course they did not. They hadn't even heard about reservations, let alone made one. They looked at each other. What was a 'reservation'?

Nonetheless, they were assured there would be no problem as the restaurant wasn't busy and were promptly ushered to a table. Above the table, a crystal chandelier lighted the area.

"Nice stuff," said Bob and Ben agreed.

When asked if they would like drinks, both ordered Cokes. They were under age for alcoholic beverages and, although they would have liked some, decided not to take a chance. Identification may be requested and they would be denied alcohol anyway. For a main course, they ordered ribs for Ben, and chicken for Bob, all delivered by a white gloved waiter with perfect manners.

Prior to the main entry, two stemmed crystal cups arrived at the table, a lemon wedge on each rim.

"Did we order drinks?" Bob asked.

Thinking little of the question Ben assured his friend they had not.

"Well, we got 'em," Bob continued. "I guess we're in luck."

Still Ben thought nothing of Bob's comments as he sat and worked on his Coke.

Precisely as the waiter arrived with the main course, Bob lifted his glass to his mouth to take a drink of the cherished liquid out of the crystal cup. He had no idea what type of drink it was but assumed it was wine or a martini. Whatever it was, he was going to enjoy it. He felt mature. Besides, they had heard of such things being served in fancy restaurants.

Midway through placing the meals on the table, the waiter froze. He stifled a laugh and fought with a smile but was eventually overcome by emotion. He neither laughed nor smiled; but emitted what seemed to be a sneeze, hurriedly placed the plates on the table and headed for the kitchen, laughter finally finding its way out of his throat.

Ben looking around to locate the source of the chuckle let his gaze fall on a very red faced Bob.

Bob had taken a huge swallow of water—from his finger bowl!

Watermelon Whine

As they were want to do, Ben and Marv found themselves on the road, hungry for a treat and in the middle of nowhere. Finding themselves in watermelon country, the treat of the day would most certainly be watermelon.

Heat and dust had taken their toll as the pair of handsome heroes had made their way over country roads in search of a haven for the night. Often, sleeping facilities included a sleeping bag on the ground as each of the adventurers took their place on opposite sides of the small sports car, their pride and joy. But last night's drama, accompanied with their grime and thirst had forced them to reassess their finances to determine if a hostel, or even a hotel, and a shower could be worked into the debit column and leave a balance to cover gasoline. Work was an option but came about only when the duo found themselves in dire straits. They much preferred dining on homemade Ketchup soup to work.

This morning had been different, however. Upon retiring, the pair worried only about thieves who may come in the night and lift gear from the sports car, whose top was never in the up position. Therefore, sleeping arrangements was a top of the list of their security measures. Thought of bodily harm never entered their minds. But, they had awakened to an unexpected interloper who could have caused them harm. As they opened their eyes and peered beneath the car at each other, a stranger appeared between them.

There, curled up nicely under the engine, enjoying any heat it could gain on the cool morning was a Diamond Back Rattler.

Carefully, extracting themselves from their sleeping bags and wondering if they had sleeping partners to share their body heat, the pair made their way to their feet. Inspection showed no bed partners.

Ignoring any doors on the sports car, Ben and Marv tossed their sleeping bags, unrolled, into the back seat, vaulted over doors, started the engine and turned for the road, leaving their camp mate as far behind as possible.

Yes! If that's the type of friendships they would make in this area of the country, they would opt for indoor accommodations tonight. It would damage the budget but at the very least allowed time to resolve some questions and to familiarize themselves with problems they may face in this unknown countryside.

Whether a shower or watermelon were placed higher on their list of priorities fell by the wayside as they passed a melon stand. Communicating without words, as so often happened with the well traveled pair, Ben turned into the stand.

Having grown up far away from watermelon land, the pair simply stood and stared at the hundreds of water melons on display. Remembering ladies who tapped the melons in supermarkets where he grew up, Ben thought tapping may add some clue to choosing a melon successfully. He had no idea why they tapped melons and had no idea what he was supposed to hear or feel. Were they to be firm, sound hollow or whatever the clue might be, he could only hope something would come out of the tapping.

Tap he did. But to his ears, each and every melon sounded and felt exactly the same. Soon Marv joined in the exercise, not having the slightest clue of what they were doing. Twenty melons later, still none jumped forward yelling, "Pick me!"

Engaged in his tapping, Ben had not noticed the elderly gentleman who appeared by his shoulder and jumped as the stranger spoke.

"Whatcha doin'?" he asked.

Ben did his best to explain the situation, outlining both his needs and trying to reassure himself that he was using the correct procedure. He also went on to talk about the rattler and their plans for the night.

"Well," drawled the stranger, "you can come on home with me an' do some cleanin' up. But first, I'd better be showin' you boys somethin' 'bout pickin' melons."

"First thing," he went on, "Yer at the wrong place."

"Wrong place?" the young men thought. "How could we be at the wrong place? We want a watermelon and there they are. What's this old bird talking about."

With a stride as leisure as his drawl, the stranger made his way to a solitary box of the most horrific melons anyone ever laid eyes on.

He bent, moved several solid colored melons aside and reached below, coming up with the ugliest, striped melon in the box.

"Choosin' a melon's like pickin' a wife," drawled the old timer.

"First, ya gotta have the strippity ones. They's the only ones what's any good. Then ya look for these here **fork** marks."

"See," he went on holding the natural disaster up for careful inspection.

"Ya see boys, she's just like people. This here melons bin hit by forks and gone through a tough life. But like people, the uglier she is on the outside, the sweeter she is on the inside."

"An they's ready fer more than eatin' too," he concluded.

Ben and Marv had no idea what the last comment was all about but followed their new friend home as promised. There he sliced the melon he'd chosen. It was, as he had said, undoubtedly the best they had ever experienced.

Reaching under the counter, the water melon expert extracted a jug.

"An this here's what theys also good fer," he said as he poured the jug's contents into glasses.

"Have sit," he went on handing each of his young friends a glass.

With a glass of watermelon wine in one hand, a slice of water melon in the other, Ben and Marv drifted into oblivion, certain they had found heaven.

As for the shower, what shower? One should never take a chance on disrupting paradise.

What's on Tap

Cruisin' was the norm. Take a hot car, a nice summer evening, an A&W drive-in and how could life get better. All the hot cars met at 'the dub' to swap tales and set up a few drags just to ensure one had the fastest car. If the car happened to be a convertible—so much the better.

Roy was fortunate. He had it all, as far as his friends and the ladies could see. He was tall, good looking, had a large engine under the hood of his convertible and all the lines one could imagine when it came to meeting young ladies. Saying he was popular around town would be an understatement. Yes, he had it all.

Roy's Lincoln convertible was not the fastest street monster in town, but no one knew that fact for certain. He never raced with the other cars. He merely passed off the suggestion with an off the cuff comment, "Nah! Don't wanna race. Gotta have more of a challenge before I turn loose the horses."

Only his friends knew the truth. Others tended to believe his explanations and often shied away from suggesting a drag at all, not wanting to be embarrassed when they failed the test. In fact, Roy's Lincoln was exactly like its owner, more show than substance. He cruised slowly, pretending to enjoy the evening, the scenery and whatever lady he had riding with him on a pretext. He had established himself as an unknown entity and no one wanted to find out the truth.

Under the hood of the Lincoln, it appeared to have the horses to get the job done in a drag race. Chrome and carburetors seemed to be everywhere. But the horses under the hood were lame. The only impressive action coming from them was the thunder that was released through a pair of special and expensive mufflers and tailpipes.

Roy's friends were often pulled over by police cruisers and checked out. They were rarely ticketed as they knew the safest place to hold their drag races, right in front of the police station on Seventh Avenue. Whether the police failed to patrol the area or not, was not a question. Perhaps they felt it was the safest place to drag as they knew it would happen and could observe the action easier from a window. It rarely brought an officer to the curb.

Roy was simply not involved in the racing. He preferred cruising down one street and up another, either searching for young ladies who would like to cruise along or even another convertible. Should a convertible be the case, Roy and his friend Ben always had a ball in the car and the two vehicles would cruise along playing catch from car to car.

Roy had two failures. First, he hated tailgaters which often led to trouble and second, he liked ladies. Should a car follow him closely, he habitually slammed on his brakes to cause the tailgater, grief. With months of this activity behind him, he chose to slam on the brakes once too often. He was hit from behind and, much to his amazement, the car behind him turned on flashing lights. He'd been hit by a police cruiser.

Roy, in his inimitable manner jumped out and began to harass the officer telling him he was automatically in the wrong for tailgating. And if that wasn't enough of a problem, a second cruiser sat behind the first, lights flashing and parked in the trunk of the first. There stood an undaunted Roy, now demanding that each officer ticket the other and he, of course, had no fault in the accident. No tickets were handed out but one black Lincoln was followed wherever it was seen for months to come.

The Lincoln had one modification that appeared on no other car of the time and its driver was extremely proud of developing the special feature. On the dashboard were four switches and, neatly hidden beneath the dash, were four tiny nozzles. They were the answer to why his glass of root beer never seemed to go empty. Only the ladies who cruised with him were aware of the Lincoln's special feature.

On parking to overlook the city with a young lady, Roy would turn and ask, "Could I offer you a drink?"

The reply was usually in the affirmative as his date expected a cola.

"Will that be whisky, rum, vodka or gin," Roy would continue.

Thinking the entire affair a joke, the date of the evening would choose one. Roy would calmly hold a glass under the dashboard and turn a switch, filling the glass with premixed liquor carried by a hose from the hidden bottles in his trunk. A simple windshield washer motor had created an undetectable, portable bar.

As with all things, Roy's lifestyle was bound to change. The day of the cruiser and the playboy would end for him. It was a matter of time until his destiny took its course. Cruising Main Street one fall evening, he spotted a most beautiful young lady standing in line to purchase movie tickets. Pulling to a stop at the curb, the Lincoln driver put his arm on top of the passenger seat and leaned over.

"It's a nice night for a movie," he began, "but a nicer one to just cruise around town. Would you like to come for a ride?"

Although a bit surprised, the young lady agreed to cruise. She could see the movie the next evening. She hopped aboard.

At the very first stop light, Roy's ego kicked in.

"How would you like to stay at my place tonight?" he asked.

The couple had their first disagreement. "I wouldn't," she replied.

As calmly as before, Roy got out of the driver's door, walked around the vehicle and opened the other door for the young lady to get out. She didn't.

Roy had met his match. He had a lady who was not interested in joining him at home, even to watch a movie and one who refused to leave his car. He was beside himself. He had no idea what to do to solve the situation.

The young lady, on the other hand knew exactly what to do. Three months later, the couple was married.

Reserved Decision

Eighteen, bored and invincible, Ben was in search of new experiences in his life. And his best friend Ron seemed to have the answer. The pair would join the reserve army, get a part time pay-cheque and have some fun along the way.

Finding their way to the reserve's armory, they advanced to the office of the commandant – a major.

"We'd like to join the reserves," Ron told the commander. "What do we have to do?"

The clear reply seemed easy enough.

"If you're not eighteen, you have to get your parents permission in writing," said the major. "There's a form here for that."

"Oh we don't need the form," replied Ron, "we're both old enough."

"Then all you have to do is fill out this form and sign it and you're in," the major assured them, passing each one a form.

It was the simplest procedure the two boys could imagine. They filled in the pertinent information and signed on the appropriate line.

Finally, Ben had a question.

"This is a tank unit, right?" he asked.

Assured that the unit was indeed an armored unit which consisted of tanks, Ben felt he'd hit the big time. He would learn to fire the big guns, fire machine guns, even drive tanks. Plus he was assured an automatic summer job and travel.

He clarified the point with the commander. But this time the reply was far less assuring than the previous one had been.

"Sure! You'll get to do all that, right after basic training," the major assured him.

"Basic training, with marching, running and all that stuff?" Ben asked while attempting to ready himself for the answer. It was affirmative.

"But when will that happen, and where?" he asked. "We're both in school."

"That isn't a problem at all," said the major. "You'll be sent to a military camp to take basic training next summer. If you pass it all, including unarmed combat, you'll come back home for school, then spend the next summer training on tanks unless they decide to place you with another unit."

The whole idea of fighting was displeasing to Ben. Ron hadn't mentioned a thing about fighting, running or marching. None of these ranked high on Ben's list of priorities. He merely wanted to get paid and drive tanks, fire guns or spin that top piece, "what was it called, a turret?"

True to his promise, the major shipped the rookies hundreds of miles from home to take basic training. They arrived in camp on a dismal rainy day and were greeted by the bleakest enclosure they had ever laid eyes upon. The greeting committee was not to their liking either. Stepping out of the bus, there he stood – the Monster from Hell.

On his arm, three stripes could be seen and they were the closest thing to an emotion the monster displayed. He stood stiffly, a broom stick surely placed where his backbone should have been or at least in that general area and showed no sentiment, no expression on his weathered face whatever.

The monster spoke.

"I'm Sergeant Cunningham," it said. "It won't take long until you get the idea of this camp. You'll learn to respect my orders, respond to my orders and hate me in very short order. Now find your assigned bunks on the double and report to the drill square."

Ben had no trouble believing Cunningham. He already detested the sergeant and hate would be a very small step forward. The drill square was out of the question. He'd just finished twelve hours of a very cramped bus ride and he was tired. He wanted to find his bunk, but he also wanted to use it, and right now!

The two found their bunks easily enough and were pleased to learn they were upper and lower on the same unit.

"Just for one minute," Ben told his friend, "I have to lie on this thing and close my eyes."

Ron climbed to the top bunk and decided to stretch out, but there was no way he would fall asleep as he feared Ben might. He was more experienced with the military and preferred to be in the sergeant's good books. He was soon to be merely called Cunningham when speaking about him.

Moments later, the rookies were surprised to learn that Cunningham could, indeed, change his facial expression. A bellow to shake the pair from their bunks and their open eyes found them staring at a very red-faced sergeant, standing stock-still with his hands on his hips.

"You two can forget the drill square for now," he told the rookies.

That sounded very good to Ben. At last he would get some needed sleep with drill cancelled.

"Come with me," beckoned the sergeant. "This is where we separate the men from the boys. You are about to be introduced to your first and most important piece of military weaponry."

A short visit to the supply office and Ron and Ben found themselves issued military knives. Obviously, they would take unarmed combat or something like that instead of drill. The army seemed to move in strange and mysterious ways and have difficulty making up its mind. Or perhaps it was only this particular sergeant that had memory problems.

Passing down a hallway and through a door, Ben was prepared to start training.

"Is this where we begin our training?" he asked, beginning to feel excitement creep upon him.

"It is!" Sergeant Cunningham replied, calmly pointing to a mountain formed from bags of potatoes. "Get started boys. When the bags are empty it should be time for that nap you wanted."

"Point taken," Ben thought. "I won't cross this guy again. We'll peel the spuds and everything will return to normal."

Wrong!

By the time the potatoes were peeled and their heads touched pillows the other recruits had enjoyed a few hours sleep. It seemed their eyes had barely closed when the bellow came again.

"C'mon you lazy louts," came the bellow. "Let's get up and at 'er. It's four in the morning and time for a little road work. A few of you think this is a kiddy summer camp so let's go out and have some fun. Full pack, ten minutes in front of the motor pool."

The monster turned on its heel and departed.

"Well," Ben said, "that didn't take long. He said we'd hate him and I've already got a pretty good head start on that one."

In front of the motor pool sat Cunningham, one leg hanging over the side of a jeep with a bull horn in his right hand. He even had a chauffeur.

"Move out!" he ordered. "Twenty miles on the double down that road. You'll know when you finish, you'll be back here."

Slipping and sliding in the mud on the road, the platoon headed out at a trot. From the faces of the troop when they chanced to look at Ben and Ron, the future would not be friendly.

Over the next six weeks of their stay in Hell, there were to be many more runs. Dirty pipes which left dust on inspecting officer's white gloves, beds made improperly, and kits packed incorrectly, all meant a night time visit from the camp monster. The squad was beginning to wonder if the monster ever slept. But then, he could always be grabbing naps between yelling on his stupid bull horn as he rode along in a jeep, urging on the runners.

The day finally arrived when advanced training would take place. The platoon was informed the conditioning section of their training was complete, no more running, no more obstacle courses. Today, they would take live fire training.

"At last!" Ben told Ron. "Now we get to at least fire something."

They didn't. Live fire training did not mean they would be firing guns. It meant they would be learning to live with bees buzzing over their heads, learning to keep those heads down.

It was an unbelievable situation. Each time there was a rifle report, another of those darn bees flew past. Getting shot at was also not in the plan of the two would be soldiers.

Six weeks in Hell complete, the summer ended with the army's idea of a party, which meant beer, beer, lots of beer. Unfortunately, one recruit had learned to hate his sergeant more than was planned. He broke a beer bottle and with the broken glass in hand, attacked Cunningham. Without thinking, Ben hit him over the head with a pool cue, knocking him to the floor and breaking his weapon.

"I can't believe I did that," he said looking around. "I've learned to hate you sergeant, as you said I would. But somehow you have my respect as well. I have the feeling, in battle, you'd be the first one over the hill."

The camp Monster broke a smile.

"And that," he said, looking at Ben, "is what it's all about soldier. We may hate each other, but we sure will look after each other as well."

The boys understood. They had learned to respond to orders without question. By being the meanest man they had ever met, Cunningham was sending a bus load of men home, where only boys had arrived.

Tanked

Basic training had ended for the members of the army reserve unit. It was time to return to their homes and hope for better things. Ron and Ben had joined the reserve unit for a summer job and fun. So far it had been anything but fun.

To end the summer, they were sent to an active army base for further training. Both felt they had enough training for one summer but neither wished to throw in the towel, give up or admit failure. They could take it.

Much to their pleasure, they discovered, upon arrival, that they would be driving tanks at last, or taking part in live fire maneuvers and firing guns. This was what they had in mind when they signed on with the reserve unit in the first place. But what would be the first thing they saw when their bus arrived at the camp? The Monster in the form of Sergeant Cunningham greeted them. But he was smiling, greeting the boys on the bus as regular soldiers—almost as equals. Ben knew better. No one was an equal to Cunningham. He was a born leader who demanded respect, didn't care if he was liked, but wanted to know his boys would follow him and feel comfortable in their roles. He needn't have worried.

The assignment started with a bang. Morning one found the troops lined up for roll call after which they were headed for the tanks, without further delay. Explanations were given and instructions on the operation of all equipment and assignments were made. Ron and Ben were assigned to the same tank crew where Ben would drive and Ron would function as the gunner.

The tank commander was a grizzled war veteran. They had little idea where all this was leading. Why the tank even needed a commander was a mystery. Would the driver not determine where they were going and the gunner do the shooting. How much more was needed?

The answers fell into place rapidly. For the gunner to be effective, two other members of the corps were needed, one to reload the gun and the second to determine angles, trajectory and turn the turret which hosted the big gun. The commander could normally be found sitting with his head out of the turret, barking directions which came through as speed or directions left and right, often in degrees. Ben had always hated degrees and geometry. He found this hard to swallow.

For Ben, driving the tank was a delight and offered no challenge as he had driven tractors and bulldozers on the farm and at a friend's business. It seemed the same. No steering wheel and operated by two sticks, some brakes and an accelerator pedal was as easy as it could be. Push the right stick forward, the tank turned left. It was simple.

For the next week, they moved the tank around, getting accustomed to every detail of its operation. Simulated firing of the gun seemed as simple as driving. Then the problems began. In combat, all things changed. Hatches were closed and no one other than the tank commander could see. Ben drove strictly from instructions and gauges. The gun found parked targets, fired live ammunition and attempted to destroy the enemy. Both driving and firing were proving tougher than expected. None of the targets were hit, let alone destroyed, and Ben was having problems of his own.

Over his radio he heard the commander.

"Watch out for the……… never mind."

He had run head-on into a tree and knocked it to the ground. The monstrous tank barely reacted but he had been distinctly told, "don't run over trees."

Enjoyment heightened when the groups were taken on bivouac. Infantry, tanks, supply units, medics, everyone took part. The tanks of course enjoyed rolling past the infantry units on the dusty roads and choking them with dust. Perhaps the Highlander units were the easiest with which to gain entertainment as they were a surly group and shouted and waved their rifles as the tanks passed.

To Ben, the Highlanders were even more interesting. On morning parades, he had watched them fall into rank wearing their kilts. In the evening, the kilts reappeared. While camped on bivouac, the kilts still appeared after the day's march. Where those kilts were during the day, only the Highland units knew. Yet they were always present.

With the women's army corps in camp, the final day was one of entertainment for most of the tank unit and especially for Ben. He could drive his tank where he wanted and be a complete showoff. While the ladies focused on the tank, Ron stepped down into the belly of the tank and he and Ben thrust their heads through open hatches to greet the ladies and wave as the tank sped by.

Unfortunately, Ben was more interested in watching the women than watching the direction in which he was taking the tank. Before he could make any decision, let alone, adjustments, the tank went over a river bank and came to rest on the bottom of the channel. Water rushed in turrets and the engines died. Eight or ten feet of water were just too much for the clanking beast.

As the crew swam to shore, they were met by the infamous Sergeant Cunningham. Before the sergeant could even speak Ben had only one thing to say.

"Ok Sarg, where's the spuds."

Gassed

Ben and his friends were suffering a fuel shortage.

That was the problem Ben, Wayne and Jerry were experiencing on a chilly, November night in a small town in the high country. It wasn't that the service stations were closed. Indeed, they weren't. But there was a fuel shortage in the gas tank of their car. Here they were with Jerry's car, dates waiting; no fuel in the tank and not enough money in their pockets to pay admission to a movie and buy gas. It was a conundrum of the highest level.

"Do you have a Mexican credit card in the car?" Ben asked his friend.

Jerry looked confused.

"What's that?" was all he said.

A brief explanation and Jerry understood it was a five foot piece of hose, a can for gas and some suction, usually supplied by the mouth.

"Oh," he said, "You mean we should siphon some from another car."

"Right on!" Ben replied.

Jerry expressed his concerns over the issue in terms of 'stealing' but knew where to find a hose and gas can. There was an old hose in his father's garage, along with an empty can that would do just fine.

Ben and Wayne calmed Jerry's concerns about stealing by assuring him that it wouldn't really be stealing if they took the gas from his father's car.

The trip home had positives and negatives. The hose was there, the can was there but there was no car in sight. They chose another site for the upcoming crime. Ben's house was targeted.

Luck was with them. There sat the family car in the yard with no one around. They opened the gas tank, inserted the hose and told Jerry to begin sucking on it. It was his credit card. He should use it.

Jerry sucked, sucked and sucked some more but was unsuccessful in his attempt. Soon he had inhaled enough gas fumes to make him ill but none of the liquid was being drawn out of the tank. He headed for the bushes.

"It must be nearly empty," Ben said. "He leaves it that way a lot. I guess we head for your place Wayne."

Desperation was taking over. The gas gauge in Jerry's car had been registering empty for quite some time. And the clock was moving along. They would be late to pick up their dates.

Wayne's family kept their car in a garage but this offered little problem. In this town, no one locked their doors. They would open the big door and get to work. Five minutes tops and they would be ready to cruise.

Jerry pulled up in the driveway feeling quite at home, Wayne opened the garage door and Ben grabbed the hose and can. Wayne's father greeted them.

"Having a nice evening boys?" he enquired.

Jerry froze, Ben hid the hose and can behind his back and Wayne assured his father everything was going just fine.

"I just came out to tune up the old car, maybe wash it and polish it too," Wayne's father said, being obvious to list a few hours of work. They knew, he knew.

Excusing themselves, they hit the road once again.

"We can't be much longer," said Ben. "I guess we have to hit the semi parked over by the stockyards. We're only after a little gas, they'll never miss it."

Ben's watch showed eight thirty and they were to pick up their ladies at nine. Time was of the essence.

The car hidden they made their way to the semi trailer unit. Things were going well. Sure, it was stealing but only a little. Didn't the size of the theft count for anything?

Ben reached for the cap to the gas tank as Wayne's voice came clearly through the crisp night air.

"Holstein," was all he said.

"In the corrals?" Jerry asked, thinking of cows.

Jerry had never been the sharpest knife in the drawer. He was slow on the pick up at times.

"He means cops," Ben said. "Under the truck and get behind a wheel."

Ben wondered why he traveled with Jerry at all. He was slow to react and often didn't even read situations accurately, if at all.

The black and white cruiser passed slowly, shining a flashlight here and there around the truck as it went. But it passed. Then it passed again and again. For hours the cruiser circled. The boys hid under the truck and chilled without jackets, worrying about getting caught and being late for their dates.

The cruiser pulled up and stopped. A window opened on the passenger side.

"Aren't you guys getting a little cold?" asked the police officer. "It's a bit chilly to be lying on the ground without jackets. Now why don't you just crawl out of there and into the back seat of our car? It's nice and warm in here."

They'd been toyed with. The police had known they were there the entire time.

They crawled out, bones stiffening and teeth chattering and entered the police cruiser.

"There you go," said the officer. "Now you can just ride around with us a while, get warm and maybe help us find some kids we heard were trying to steal some gas."

The boys knew they were caught.

It was four in the morning when the officers offered to give the boys a "lift" home. This was not something they were looking forward to. That lift was going to have consequences at the end, and they knew it. But at least they weren't headed for jail.

Ben was dropped off first. He and an officer went to the door where Ben attempted to thank him for his help and the ride. But the officer wasn't that easy to be rid of.

"Ben," he said. "I think I'll have to knock and speak with your Dad. It's late and he may have been worried. I have to tell him it was all my fault or you may get in trouble, get grounded or something."

He knocked on the door, finally bringing a very groggy father to the door. In minutes, he explained the situation, and he wasn't telling about his part, only Ben's. Ben knew he wouldn't be going out on dates for a while and would certainly not use the family car.

As the officer turned to walk away, he had a parting comment. "By the way," he said, "the next time you need gas, don't pick on a semi. Big trucks run on diesel and that could ruin a gas engine."

Ben was devastated. He'd suffered the entire ordeal for nothing and missed a date. Wayne and Jerry, who had been listening, were white faced as they were sure their fate would be the same as Ben's.

Two days later, the trio met at school and discussed the outcome of the evening. All were grounded for a month, Jerry lost use of his own car and they were afraid to meet the girls they had stood up. They'd be pretty angry.

Much to the surprise of the boys, their dates met them in a very jovial manner, smiling and friendly.

It seems Gord had come by with some friends and they had gone to the movie after all. As they walked away, one lady stopped, looked back and said, "By the way guys, Gord will be coming by next weekend too."

Lorriane Fee

When in trouble, Les pulled out the heavy artillery

Les is More

There he sat. Eighty six years old and he was displaying his four most recent gold medals, captured in his last track outing.

The most valuable lessons in life are often learned from the quiet, unpretentious leader who lives right next door. One may be totally oblivious to any leadership skills, until they open their eyes one day to discover the best lessons are learned from the most quiet, unexpected sources. Leadership is often set by example.

Les was such a man. He spoke slowly, had a sense of humor somewhat off the beaten path. He was always late and exhibited forgetfulness throughout his life. When suggested that he lead a group, be the heavy handed father with his family, the final authority, be outgoing, teach a lesson or set an example it seemed certain he would fall short of the mark. He never did. He set a fine example for his children and anyone near.

Les went through each day as quietly and as unobtrusive as he possibly could. It was impossible for him to take control of any situations. Indeed, he was more likely to forget an appointment or where his car was parked than exert authority.

Nonetheless, he retained a certain ability to take charge without being imperious in his demeanor. As a track star in high school and a reputable tennis player, he went largely unnoticed by onlookers. Yet competitors were well aware of his inherent abilities as he took charge of the track or the tennis courts. When it came to a field of interest, he was extremely competitive while remaining what everyone called "a good sport".

But, was he a good sport beneath the surface and behind his friendly smile? Only his closest friends would ever have guessed that he was driven to win and losing was acceptable but far from desirable.

Off the track, he rarely took on an aggressive role. It simply was not in his nature. However, hearing through town gossip that the young lady of his dreams was dating someone and the relationship could lead to marriage, Les had no alternative but to act. He wanted her for his wife and would not allow her to slip through his fingers without putting up a fight. If he didn't try, he would regret the missed opportunity forever.

As the party rolled around Les' princess attended with her beau. Les was not on the guest list, but having heard a proposal of marriage could be in the offing, he did what he had to do. He crashed the party.

Much to his surprise and relief, as he opened his heart to the lady of his dreams who he hoped to make his queen, he discovered a mutual love. Taking her by the hand, he whisked her away from the party, her date, and the altar. The pair eloped, disappointing the bride's parents, and married that very night.

As the years passed, seven children resulted from the outcome of his spontaneous actions. But spontaneity was not always the case with Les, as his wife, Dorothy, seemed far more outgoing. She knew his every move and acted upon them. She enjoyed being in control of her family and often warned her children, as a last resort, of the heavy hand of their father when he returned from work each evening. However, the family inevitably sat down to the evening meal, still waiting for the heavy hand to fall.

With the older children in the lead, baiting their younger siblings, the meal became nothing less than pandemonium.

At last, Dorothy could stand it no more.

"Les," she would blurt in obvious frustration. "Speak to the children!"

True to his nature, Les would calmly raise his head, survey the activities at the table and speak.

"Oh! I'm sorry," he'd say. "Hi Kids!" and calmly return to his meal.

Family was important and, in Les' mind, identifying with his children was of the utmost importance. Whether slot car racing, swimming, or a summer water fight, he took part, if indeed, he wasn't the instigator. In the early stages, his loving wife looked on in amusement, but the activities normally got to the point of frustration.

Once all seven children, some now young adults, formed a coalition to ensure their father was near drowning, Les was forced to bring out the heavy artillery. Grabbing the garden hose, turning it on full force, he pushed his adversaries to full retreat. The former assailants rushed into the house for asylum. Undaunted, Les followed, hose and all, and much to his wife's distress took his revenge indoors.

For a time, life slowed considerably. Less found one knee far too painful to allow exercise. A visit to his doctor confirmed his worst fears. There was cartilage damage and it would have to be completely removed.

"Just cut away the torn tissue," he argued but such would not be the case. The entire cartilage was removed and the patient was directed to use crutches for the coming six months, possibly longer.

Some weeks later, a family friend was to be married on a beach in the beauty of the outdoors. The crutches were of little use and sank into the sand every time he moved. Being a determined man, he would attend the ceremony. But the crutches caused a problem. He merely threw them into the bushes, never to be seen again, and limped his way over the beach.

Not until the age of seventy and yet another knee operation, would Les finally set his sights on world fame. It wasn't his plan, but it was his destiny. He decided to return to his high school passion of running.

And it seemed to be a developmental stage for the upcoming senior star. He competed and developed, taking part in fun runs and marathons. Eventually, after passing eighty, he became a world champion at four events, four hundred, eight hundred, fifteen hundred and five thousand meters. What did this mean to the new hero?

Of course, it meant pride in his accomplishment. But when entering a track meet and hearing himself introduced as a world champion in his age category, his first reaction was to look around to see where the champion would be. Then, suddenly realized it was he who was being introduced, and making an appearance. All five foot four, hundred pounds soaking wet, gangly legged and smiling, he would make his entrance.

Les was a teacher, an example and presented a goal for which anyone should strive. For many, it takes a lifetime to set an example. For Les, he spent a lifetime setting examples.

Run Chicken Run

It was Friday night. They had a car, dates and no money to go to the drive-in movies. There was only one way out. This night would have to be a chicken roast down by the river. Still money remained a problem. Where would the chickens come from?

Ben, Gord, Wayne and Larry checked for chicken at home. For eight people, they had decided they'd need four. Ben even requested the privilege of taking four from his own families flock and cleaning them for the occasion. Permission was withheld.

Only one recourse was left – theft. They would have to wait until after dark and raid someone's chicken coop. Ben suggested his Uncle Clarence was the best target as his hen house was far from any living quarters. Until then, at least the car had gas in the tank and they could take part in one of their favorite things, cruising.

With nightfall, the gangsters and their dates made their way to the uncle's farm, parked and headed across a field for their target. The hens would be roosting and locked away inside. It would be easy-picking. Ben and Gord were chosen as the thieves while the remainder of the party waited in the getaway car, Wayne was the designated driver.

Entry to the unlocked henhouse presented no problem and they were certain they had not been detected from the house. The two passed along the rows of roosts, touching chickens and trying to choose only the best. They should be young and tender and, of course, healthy and fat. Each touch of a chicken brought forth a small protest which was passed on to the rest of the flock. The hens became noisier and noisier until the entire hen house was in an uproar.

Voices in the yard were heard and they were getting closer.

"Must be a coyote or something bothering the hens," the voice said.

The reply sent chills up the spines of the chicken thieves.

"I've got the gun," a second voice replied.

That was all the encouragement the boys needed to burst into action. Grabbing a chicken by the legs, one in each hand, they passed through the door running, knocking cackling hens from their perches and nearly trampling them in the stampede.

"Chicken thieves," said the first voice.

On a dead run, the pair crossed the chicken yard, put one foot on top of a rail fence and ran over it, heading into the night with their prizes. They expected to hear a shot ring out, none came. They would make it.

Ben knew they had to make it. He was not his uncle's favorite nephew and, if he was caught, the repercussions could be devastating.

Only on reaching the car did the pair look back. They hurled four live chickens into the vehicle and followed them. The crime was a success and the prizes were in hand. Now it was time to go to the river, butcher, clean the hens and roast them on an open fire.

With Wayne behind the wheel, Larry proving to be afraid of chickens and Gord and Ben completely out of breath, controlling the hens fell to the girls. They calmed the excited hens by setting them on their knees and stroking them.

A few miles down gravel roads, passing through trees, and they would be at their destination. No one seemed to be following or they would have seen headlights behind. Wayne slowed to a safe speed and the party-goers took on a jovial attitude.

The river beckoned, the trees opening their arms to the night picnickers. They were safe, protected, and dinner was in their hands. Ben removed an axe and knife from the trunk of the car and searched for a chopping block. Hens had to be prepared before they could meet their demise. With water in the river for cleaning, all that was necessary was an axe, a chopping block and a butcher knife. They were prepared. All the tools for a chicken roast were at hand.

Once the chickens would have been roasted and devoured, blankets spread on the sand would be the perfect end to the evening. Each couple would have their own space and settle down to watch the stars. Cuddling close was merely a bonus.

But it seemed the ladies had grown rather fond of their traveling mates and refused to give them up. They had become pets. They would far sooner cuddle with their feathered friends than their boy friends. The party had now grown from eight to twelve. Nothing would be eaten. They would simply enjoy the ripple of the river and relax.

Blankets were spread and trios (a boy, a girl and a hen) lay back to watch the stars.

Not knowing what to do with the chickens other than to return them, the party headed back for the uncle's farm. There was no need to enter the hen house as sunrise would soon be upon them. Nor did they wish to find themselves trapped.

Parking as close as possible to the farm, while avoiding detection, it was once again up to Ben and Gord to venture cross country to the hen yard. Reaching their destination, they calmly placed the hens in the chicken yard and left a prepared note pinned to the hen house door.

"Dates were hard to find," it read. "Thanks for loaning us some ladies."

Dialing Paws

Twenty one years of age and already a supervisor for the telephone company, Ben was a rising star; of this there was no doubt. He had little to do personally other than organize the dozen girls who worked in the office, offering service to the public.

Of course, there were minor issues to clear up. He had complaints regarding the company or staff directed to him. They were easy problems, usually very simple.

Receiving a telephone call from an irate motel owner asking when his new switch board would be installed, there was only one question.

"What switchboard?" Ben asked.

"The one I bought from a salesman last week. It was less expensive than the ones you rent so I decided to own it. Now I want it hooked up," was the reply.

"Unfortunately, sir," said Ben, "We don't install any switch boards but those owned by the telephone company and we don't hook other boards to our lines. The only thing we can do to help is to buy the board for four hundred dollars, ensure it is in proper working order and rent it back to you."

"Four hundred bucks!" the motel owner screamed. "That's less than half what I paid for it! I'll go to the competition."

"As you wish, sir," was Ben's response as he hung up the telephone. He knew he'd be getting a call back shortly.

In moments, a very embarrassed motel owner called again. "There is no competition is there?" he asked.

"Nope," Ben replied, "only us. So when would you like us to pick up that switchboard and see if it complies with our standards?"

More difficult problems arose concerning the manner in which his staff handled the public. The company may have a monopoly but being friendly and courteous was essential. He had stressed this in many staff meetings.

Therefore, he was taken by surprise when he received a complaint regarding the decorum of one of his ladies, Cindy.

"She was downright rude!" said the lady caller. "I explained the whole situation and she just became rude."

Ben asked for clarification.

"Well," said the caller, "I was on holiday for six weeks and during that time, someone made long distance calls from my home telephone."

"I don't see how that could happen," Ben began…

His caller cut him off. "Listen," she said, "there was nobody in the house except my puppy."

Now it all made sense. A dog could not be left alone for six weeks without someone taking care of it. He had the answer. But before he could explain, he was cut off again.

"I explained this to that Cindy girl," blurted the lady who seemed to have come upon the same answer as Ben. "And do you know what she said?"

Ben admitted he didn't.

"That rude young lady looked me straight in the eye when I told her no one was in my house and said, "Madam, does your doggy dial?"

Ben had no idea how the conversation ended. He was too busy drying tears of laughter from his eyes.

Lorriane Fee

No Sir! We always park on someone's lawn

Carnanigans

It was the perfect summer day for a drive. There was no other way to put it. An hour's drive took one to the mountains and an hour brought them back. It had to be done.

Ben, Marv and Bob crawled into Ben's old Triumph sports car, top down, and headed west for the mountains. Bob sat in the back on an unpadded jump-seat but was enjoying the breeze while the car crawled through the traffic on their way out of the city. Marv and Ben traveled everywhere together so Bob, as the newcomer, was odd-man-out and relegated to the back. He cared not. There was more wind in the back and a greater sensation of speed as the little car sped along the highway. The fact that Ben always went over the speed limit helped immensely.

Traveling down a modern highway, it took little time to reach the first mountain town. Tourist season was at its height and the scenery, the boys had come to see, was walking along the streets. A few passes and they found company to join them.

However, the joy of the day was soon dampened. A police cruiser pulled the Triumph to the curb and issued a threat.

"Get everyone out of the back seat," the officer demanded, "or I'll issue you a restricted driving ticket for restricted driving."

Ben was not only confused but on the verge of anger. When asking the officer to please tell him what 'restricted driving' was and pointing out that the car had a back seat, he received no answer. He did, however, ask his passengers to remove themselves from the 'back-seat', giving them instructions to walk the two blocks to the local police station where he intended to gain clarification.

Walking in the front door, the first person Ben noticed was a police sergeant standing behind the counter. He approached.

"Excuse me sir," he began, "Can you please tell me what 'restricted driving' is?"

The sergeant merely looked puzzled. He had no answer.

"Why do you want to know that?" he asked.

Ben gratified him with a reply, "We were driving along and an officer pulled us over and threatened to ticket us for 'restricted driving'. I've never heard of it and wanted to know what we were doing wrong."

Instead of receiving an answer, this time Ben found himself being lectured.

"You just want to cause trouble," the sergeant roared. "You city kids come out here and do nothing but cause trouble."

Now Ben was angry. He lost his composure - completely.

"If we wanted to come here to cause trouble, would we be here asking what we were doing wrong?" he shouted at the sergeant. "All I want to know is if I can have people ride in the back seat of my car or if I can't. I don't want to break any laws but I don't think I did."

He turned on his heel and exited.

"C'mon," he said to his friends, "let's get back to the city."

The drive to the mountains on a straight super highway had been fast, but not enjoyable. The sports car was engineered for curves and curves it would be.

"We'll take the old road home along the river," he told his passengers. "Then we'll have a little fun and get the feel of the road."

Pavement wound along beside the river bed with switchbacks and tight corners. Ben decelerated, accelerated, shifted gears and pushed the car to the limit. It seemed both the car and its passengers were exhilarated by the winding challenges before them.

"Now this is the kind of road we should have been on all along," Bob said from the backseat.

His comment found total agreement.

Within the hour, hair tousled from the wind, the sports car and its passengers were back in the city.

"Watch this baby," Ben said, going into a ninety degree intersection. "It's got a step down frame and I can take this at about forty.

Halfway through the corner, a sproinging sound came to the boy's ears. The steering wheel spun in Ben's hands and the car neglected to turn. It chose its own path and jumped a curb, crashed through a hedge and came to rest on a residential lawn.

Three white faced boys looked at each other in silence.

Marv was the first to speak. All he said was "lucky."

Lucky they were. Had the steering come apart earlier, the car and its occupants would have driven off a cliff and fallen to the river below.

The trio climbed from the sports car, deciding to get it one block to a nearby service station by turning the front wheels manually, when a young police officer approached. He had witnessed the entire episode.

"Having trouble?" he asked.

That, Ben thought, was the stupidest question he had ever heard. Of course he was having trouble. He'd had about enough of lectures, stupid questions and police for one day. His mouth replaced his brain.

"Not at all, officer," he replied. "I always park on lawns. The streets are too crowded."

Fortunately, the youthful officer had a sense of humor. He merely laughed at the transgression. Indeed, he proved quite helpful.

The car, the trio and the officer made their way to the service station unimpeded. Ben drove, Marv kicked one front wheel into position, Bob the other, and the officer stopped traffic.

As they rolled up on the service station lot, Ben thanked the officer who had taken the whole thing in.

"Not to worry," he replied. "I have a Triumph myself and the steering gives way all the time. Better be careful in the future, though."

Southern Comfort

New Year's Eve and a party invitation.

Ben left the house excited. Jennifer always threw great parties and he was just happy to have an invitation. The music promised to be great, there would be lots of girls with whom to dance and booze would flow. The group was under age for alcohol, but Ben knew Jennifer could always arrange the beverages.

As soon as he reached the house, Ben noticed that most of the guests had already arrived. The activities were well under way. He entered and was immediately handed a drink.

The liquid smelled wonderful and tasted good enough but burned his throat when he swallowed it. He coughed and took another sip.

"Really good stuff," he said. "What is it?"

Assured that it was expensive and called 'Southern Comfort' he determined it would be his drink for the evening. With each swallow his throat seemed to become number and as it did, the burning sensation subsided. And Ben did like the word 'expensive'.

Eventually, dancing and eating and drinking his new favorite alcohol began to take its toll. Ben became light headed, staggered through dances and became nauseous. He would have to sit for a while. All these symptoms of having a good time would pass. He knew he'd have a headache in the morning; he always did when he partied, but it was worth the pain just to have a good time.

He leaned back on the chesterfield, listening to the music. He was tired. He closed his eyes and continued to listen to the conversations and music, but something strange was happening. The room was beginning to spin.

Ben's eyes popped open. He had to stop that spinning. He'd have to lie down on the chesterfield. He did.

Lying on his back with his eyes open, Ben stared at the ceiling. Suddenly, it too began to spin. Even the chesterfield was spinning, but in the opposite direction.

Ben leapt to his feet and headed for the bathroom. He knew what was about to happen. It did. He barely made it into position before his body began to relieve itself of the cause of his illness.

"There," he said to himself, "everything will be better now."

He sat on the edge of the bath tub for a few moments just to be sure.

The next thing he knew, he heard a scuffling sound and opened his eyes. He was lying in the bath tub, staring at Jennifer's father. The party was over and it was morning.

"Well," Jennifer's father said, "at least it's nice to know you didn't cause any trouble last night. Good morning, Ben."

Ben saw absolutely nothing good about this morning. His head hurt and he was embarrassed. Grabbing his coat, he headed for the door and home without even a goodbye. It didn't feel like 'Southern Comfort' at all!

Makin' a Difference

Ben didn't set out to ask for much out of life. He didn't want to be rich and he didn't want to be famous. But there was one thing he did want and that was to make a difference.

As a high school drop out, making a difference wouldn't be easy. Setting out on the seas of life was a different matter. He could no longer stay at home. His father made that clear.

Ducking the issue of quitting school for over a week and hanging around the local billiard parlor, his father had discovered the sham. He had quit school and, therefore, the free room and board was coming to an end. Ben's father waited until the weekend, awarded him a prize of one hundred dollars with a caution to "make it last" and his brother offered him a ride to the city where he would supply room and board for one month.

It was now time for Ben to make the difference he so longed for.

His first employment found him working in the office of the local telephone company. It was considered a good job as it had a future. At first, Ben was happy but that grew into contentment. Eventually, the situation faded into one of discontentment as Ben asked himself the question, "How am I making a difference?"

Perhaps he was making a difference but didn't know it. He had risen to the position of office supervisor and had saved, at least one of the girls working with him, her job.

On this particular occasion, an irate customer had complained about her bill, accumulated during a one month holiday.

It had taken a while but Ben straightened out the problem with the customer and head office—in the end however, the young lady kept her job. But, to Ben, it didn't feel like making a difference to him.

The answer was simple, he had held the job for two years and he simply was not making a difference in his mind. He found it time to move on.

Mechanics was the answer to his problem. By helping people keep their cars running well, he would be making someone happy. That would be making a difference. But once he learned that he hated being dirty and greasy, it was time for this career choice to bite the dust. Somewhere right over the next hill, success awaited. He moved on.

When it came to hills, he noticed there were many that could be crossed and were, each and every day, by long haul truck drivers. He applied and found the questions required the use of his father's philosophy.

"Get the job," his father had said. "If you get fired after the first day, you still come out a winner. You may still be looking for a job but at least you'll have a day's pay in your pocket."

He did as advised, he lied.

"Have you ever driven a truck," was the first question.

"Sure," responded Ben who had driven farm trucks. "I can drive anything," he boasted.

To solidify his position, he offered references from as far away as he could, knowing they would never be called.

Much to his amazement, he was hired and pointed in the direction of a tractor trailer unit as a co-driver. His first excursion led into the mountains where he was certain to experience the extreme, life-on-the-edge, so to speak.

He rode and rode and finally could stand the suspense no longer.

"When will you want me to drive?" he queried.

"You won't be drivin'," said the experienced one. "Yer only here 'cause it's a company rule. Last time I let some guy drive, I was lyin' in the sleeper and heard 'im say, we're gonna hit a train,' and that sucker did."

Another dream was about to be shattered. Ben was not going to make much of a difference in this job either. He determined that when the trip was over, he'd get another job and his own truck. Little did he know that danger and excitement waited not far up the road.

While winding its way down a mountain road, the semi-tractor lost its air and brakes. Straight ahead was a Y in the road with a school yard in the middle. Children wandered everywhere, including on the roadways. Disaster was about to strike.

As the truck roared toward the intersection, Ben heard the driver command, "Hold on! We're gonna lay 'er over."

'Lay'er' over, he did. In a hail of rocks, sparks and the screaming of metal on pavement, the huge truck skidded to a stop saving the day. Shocked teachers and children looked on as their attention was drawn by the screaming metal as it slid along the road but there were no injuries.

Initially, this seemed to be just too much excitement for Ben. As he thought about it, he decided it was an omen. He had discovered the way that he could make a difference. He would become a school teacher. Perhaps the students steered clear by the sliding truck would not be the only one's he could help save and show a way to have a better life.

Through the assistance of grants, loans and jobs that ranged from working on drilling rigs to driving taxis, finishing high school and his first three years of university proved to be of little problem. However, shortly before final exams of his final year, money ran short and Ben was forced to search for night work.

Once again, he searched out a truck driving job and once again he lied. But he got the job, hauling live chickens to a processing plant at night and attending classes throughout the day. It was a tiring experience which often found him sleeping in the library. But he would manage.

Fatigue did its work as the days rolled on. Coming along a two lane highway, partially dazed from lack of sleep, he was shocked to find four headlights coming toward him. One car was passing another and he was headed for a head-on collision. He whipped the steering wheel to the right, hoping to get closer to the ditch and allow the three vehicles to pass unscathed. His effort was valiant but his planning faulty.

He dropped a trailer wheel off the highway and flipped the load. His trailer fell on its side, breaking crates and allowing their captives to spread through the fields and wander on the highway. Knowing that he must report the disaster, he called his boss in spite of the time—at two in the morning.

"Mark," he said, "I think you'd better get down here. These chickens are making some pretty funny noises."

The half asleep boss, mumbled into the phone, "Making funny noises? What do you mean?"

"Well," Ben replied, "I'm on the highway and every time a car goes by, they sort of go squish, squish."

Mark got the message quickly and was anything but impressed. The load had been flipped and chickens were running all over the road, most of them committing suicide in the headlights of passing cars.

Within the hour, the boss arrived, driving his white Cadillac and dressed in a three piece suit, complete with four hundred dollar shoes. His first comment, as he slipped through the spring mud was, "Help me catch these chickens."

"Do I still have a job," Ben asked.

There was no reply from the well dressed chicken catcher.

Ben immediately got the picture. He was unemployed again.

With his job coming to an end a certainty, Ben was not about to waste the rest of the night catching chickens. The first of his final exams was to be written in the morning and sleep would help. He climbed into the tractor which had remained on its wheels and made his way home, leaving the suited Mark to catch his chickens.

It had been an ordeal, indeed. But Ben knew none of the jobs he had held would ever help him make the difference he desired. He wanted to have an influence on the lives of others and offer a positive example.

Then it happened. The mail arrived and upon opening one letter, all he could do was stare. There it was! In large lettering, it said "Teaching Certificate" and it was made out in the name of Benjamin Bratt.

He had made it. He was a teacher and now, he would finally have the opportunity to make the difference he so much desired.

Ben headed for the teacher wanted ads in the newspaper.

It's New - Try It!

Selling is a profession few suit well. It takes ingenuity, the ability to analyze people and, at times, an aggressive attitude.

John found himself dealing with sales to retail stores. It was not something in which he had experience. Making the problem worse, he was to sell without an appointment.

"Just walk in cold, tell them what your selling, how they can make a buck and they'll buy," was his boss' only instruction.

To date, the boss was wrong. He walked in cold, introduced himself to the store manager, handed him a card and went into his spiel. It too was supposed to be a sure sale. However, whoever had written the sales' instruction manual did not anticipate the type of customer John met.

With expenses rising and sales non existent, he had to begin to make sales. His pay-cheque was based on commission. The more he sold the more money he made. His commission at this point was zero. He had worked for two weeks and was still waiting for his first sale.

His mind was set. If he sold nothing today, he would have to quit the job. He was spending his savings too fast traveling and paying his own expenses. This day would be fruitful or it was home to try something different and admit defeat. Those were two prospects he did not want to face. He liked traveling and was not good at admitting defeat. Today he would give it his all.

He believed in his product which is fundamental to all salesmen. It is difficult to sell something you could not sell to yourself. He knew his product had quality.

The first call of the morning, proved lucky. In requesting to meet the store manager, she came immediately. He often had to wait for the manager but this one was different. Perhaps it was his lucky day after all.

He introduced himself and outlined his product.

His enthusiasm was short lived. The manager made it clear that she was not interested.

"I'm sorry," she said, "but this is new to us. We've never done anything like this. I like to stay with items I know we can sell."

For John, frustration set in. He was going to come up short again. He would either quit the job or be fired at the end of the day so it may as well be now.

"So you never try anything new?" he asked the lady manager.

"Not really," was her reply. "We know what we can sell and just stick to those items."

John looked at the manager and began to make small talk.

"How many kids do you have?" he asked.

He was informed the manager had two.

"Nice kids?" John said.

"Of course," he was assured. "I'm very proud of them."

"I see," John went on. "Any grandchildren?"

The manager had five grandchildren who were the most beautiful little darlings who had ever been born. They were the pride of the lady's life.

"That's wonderful," John told the manager. "But it's a good thing you tried something new sometime in your life isn't it?"

He turned to leave, having killed his job with his sarcasm but heard a voice over his shoulder.

"Good point," she said. "We'll take six units."

Lorriane Fee

She finally found her board!

Board Lady

There he was. He was just happy to be there. This one was special. He could tell.

He met her on a blind date on New Year's Eve and just couldn't stay away from her. This lady was a keeper and he was determined to ensure it happened. She met his parents and family and they were thrilled with his latest romantic partner. Sure, she stood him up once, but his tenacity had proven the correct approach. He waited for hours until she returned home and explained herself. The explanation was enough for Ben, although the truth was she stood him up hoping he would just go away.

Now it was time to show her his roots, show her where he came from. Some twenty miles later, down country roads with snow covered fields spreading as far as the eye could see, he turned up a lane.

"This is where I grew up," he told her. "That's where the garden was and the barn was over there. It wasn't much but we loved it."

Further along the lane he pointed out sheds, hen houses, pigeon coops and finally the old deserted house.

Snow lay in the fields, it was spring and he had chosen this time of year for one specific purpose. He wanted his lady to see what it was about this place that seemed so special when he was a child. It was peaceful and serene. There was no traffic and only the odd bird flitting to and fro on the spring breezes.

A quick visit inside the tiny shack, the family had once called a house, and it was back in the car.

"We'll go to the barnyard and look out on the pasture," he said. "I want to show you something."

Turning through a gateway in the barbed wire fence, he pushed the old Ford through the small snow drifts and made his way to the top of a hill which was bordered by the barn yard. Approaching the hill top, the Ford slipped from side to side as ice formed under its wheels. It didn't matter. He grew up in the snow and could handle this type of farmyard driving.

Stopping the car just short of where the hill fell away to the west, he got out, circled the car and opened a door for his lady love. Hand in hand, they walked to the very edge of the hill.

"Close your eyes and don't open them until I say so," he told his lady.

She complied with the request.

Within a few paces, the couple stopped. Gently he took her head and turned it.

"OK," he told her, "You can open your eyes."

When the eyes opened, there was a short gasp from the young lady. Before her the hill fell away to the west. Small rivulets of water made their way through snow remaining from winter drifts and green grass was poking though in patches. Growing on the grassy spots was the beauty he had promised. Blue heads of crocuses popped up everywhere, taking centre stage in nature's spring show.

"See," he said, "That's why I like this place. It was always my favorite place. I picked crocuses here for my Mom every spring."

With those words, he began to move from one bare spot of ground to the next, bending and picking flowers until his hand held a small bouquet.

He turned and handed them to the lady of his dreams.

"Here you go," he said. "Every spring I've given these to my favorite lady. And now you're it. This is why I brought you here."

Undoubtedly, she was impressed with his romantic effort. She smiled, but never uttered a word. A simple hug was enough to get her message through.

His mission complete, the young Romeo again took the hand of his lady love and the couple made their way back to the car. The door was opened and his princess entered her golden chariot. He circled, boarded the driver's side of the black Ford, started its engine and put the car in gear. Nothing happened. The car sat in place and spun its left rear wheel. It had been parked on ice and was going nowhere fast.

"Can you drive," he asked. "I'll give it a push. It won't take much, its flat ground here."

She couldn't. But, she could push. The ground was not as flat as expected and the Ford refused to move either forward or back. It sat and spun its wheels. A new approach was needed.

A search of the farm yard turned up little in the way of helpful material. Nothing but an old board with nails was available. It would have to do.

With great effort, the nails were removed to avoid flat tires and the board jammed under the front of the spinning wheel. This would work!

It didn't. The board went under the tire well enough but was spit out behind the Ford like a toothpick. OK fine, perhaps the car could back up.

Once again, the board was put in place, but this time in back of the tire. Perhaps it would be enough to allow the car to back off the ice. Again it wasn't. The board flew out from under the hood and the car sat and spun.

"It's just throwing the board out too soon," he said. "Maybe if you stand on it, it'll stay in place long enough to help."

She did.

As soon as the car was placed in gear and he stepped on the accelerator, he would be free and they could head back to town. Of this, he was sure.

He didn't want to get moving and run over his princess who was standing behind the car on her board so he watched the rear view mirror. Stepping on the gas as gently as possible, the board once again flew past the front of the car. And his princess? Well, she just disappeared from view.

It hadn't been planned. But it turned into her first attempt at skiing. Needless to say, she wasn't up to trying the sport again, even after they were married.

Years later, she must have found her board, for she disappeared from his life forever.

Cruisin' for Trouble

It was a typical small town Saturday night. He had his first car, he had a date and there was Main Street to cruise. How could life get better? In a small town, all the elements were in place for a beautiful evening.

Toss in a milkshake, ice cream soda or a sundae and the entertainment would be complete.

For Bruce, cruising the two block length of Main Street, pulling a u-turn and idling back in the opposite direction was relatively new. Others had carried on the exercise since cars began to be spotted in North America but this was his first evening, in his first car. He felt like a 'man' behind that wheel.

The automobile has always been a source of trouble, especially so for the young man. With its first appearance, upon entering a town, a runner must run before the oily, noisy machine warning everyone of their impending doom. It could frighten horses, babies or even go out of control. An out of control automobile could do all types of damage, even run through a store front. It did travel at a breathtaking thirty miles an hour or slightly more. The car never had the right-of-way.

Since that time, little has changed in small town North America. The more notable young man still wanted to be seen, preferably with his lady love, and cruising was the way to get the job done in style. The car and the date were part of who he was, a position of pride and achievement.

Perhaps he was flying a bit too high. Bruce's confidence was as high as it could be with his left hand on the steering wheel, his right arm around the shoulders of a local beauty for all to see and his car polished to a brilliant luster. He was not about to take any nonsense from anyone. He was Bruce and, tonight, Bruce was the king of the road if not the entire town.

As luck would have it, he drew the attention of the local police. The officer following was known for being 'tough but fair'. But this was not the night for either. Bruce decided if he was pulled over he would give the man a piece of his mind. It was necessary, as his manhood in the face of a threat by the law would surely impress the lady beside him.

Several passes of Main Street later, the light flashed on the roof of the police car. The young renegade showed through as he pulled his car to the curb.

"Here he comes and is he ever going to hear about a citizen's rights," Bruce vowed to himself.

The officer strode up to the open window of the driver.

"Where you going," he asked.

"I don't see that it matters to you," was the terse reply. "I'm not breaking any laws."

As the conversation between the two continued, it became more and more heated.

"That's enough," said the officer. "Follow me to the police station."

By now Bruce was wondering whether he had impressed anyone. His lady had a white face, the officer was angry and he was just a little worried.

Leaving his car and the young lady outside while he visited a jail cell was not in his plans at all. It wasn't supposed to be that way on a small town Saturday night.

Pulling up and stopping in front of the police station, he found the officer at his driver's window once more.

"Get out!" ordered the police.

Bruce complied. Suddenly, he had become far more tolerant of the intrusion. In fact, he was gaining respect for the officer by the minute.

The policeman took a notebook from his pocket and began to look at the young man's car. Turn on this light, that light, touch your brakes and many other commands were issued and readily complied with. That cell was only steps away and there was no use taking any chances. Bruce wasn't looking through any bars yet and didn't intend to be if he had anything to say about it. Throughout the entire exercise, the officer continued to write and Bruce continued to worry. He really would prefer to stay free and at very least drive his lady home at the end of the evening.

Finally, the pen stopped moving on the note pad.

"There," said the constable, offering the note pad to the unfortunate driver. "That's a list of problems with your car that I could give you a ticket for. What do you think?"

Bruce took the notepad and looked at the list. Items numbering one through seventeen jumped out at him. He counted them just to be sure. Yes, there were seventeen all right.

"Could be pretty expensive, couldn't it?" he was asked.

Bruce had to agree.

"Yes, that's the things you could be fined for," said the officer. "You could be, but you won't. Have you learned anything here today?"

Bruce had and he admitted it. He apologized to the officer and gained more respect from the lady in the car than he had with his tough act.

In parting the policeman had one more word of advice.

"Oh Bruce," he said. "You'd better have those things fixed. You are the local mechanic."

Night Light

The sixties were open years in which a young man could grow and flourish. Fast cars, greasy hair and hob nailed boots were normal. For the other side of life, it was long hair and pacification. There were the greasers and the hippies.

Bob was a greaser. His hair was slicked back, he wore boots with metal on the toes and heels, down by the soles, and he was known to be anything but pacifistic. Indeed, he almost seemed to enjoy a good fight.

He also enjoyed fast cars. A car was a must for a young man just beginning his life. Without wheels, he was nobody. So he chose to own a Pontiac, brightly colored and with a hot engine. His other downfall was alcohol. Bob enjoyed a drink, or two, or... several.

On a warm summer night, he decided 'several' were in need and spent the early evening drinking. Well watered, he called on his friend Ben to go for a drive. Noting his condition, Ben was hesitant to get into the vehicle with his friend but, after much begging, gave in.

Cruising the streets was the way young men spent their time and Bob set out to do exactly that. He wanted to meet some young ladies. Ben, on the other hand, knew this was not a good idea in Bob's condition.

"At least, let's head out of town for a while," Ben begged.

Much to his surprise, his friend complied and headed out of town, past the city limits and down a paved highway into the countryside. This put Ben at ease for a very short time. Bob began to laugh.

"Hey, look!" he said, "We're hittin' ninety."

Ben was not impressed. But when the car-door suddenly opened, he was down right frightened. While continuing to steer the car, with one hand on the steering wheel and the other on a door handle, one foot on the gas pedal, Bob dragged his foot on the pavement.

The cleats on his boot sent sparks from the road well past the tail lights.

"Wow!" he said. "Fireworks!"

It was all a white faced, trembling Ben could take.

"Look bud," he said to his friend, "if you want to speed and you want fireworks – that's fine but how about letting me drive. You're scaring the Hell out of me."

Bob gave in, slowing the car and guiding it to the edge of the road.

"Fine," he said. "Then you drive."

Ben slid behind the wheel, feeling more comfortable. But his friend could not sit still. He crawled over his passenger seat and fell into the back seat.

"Darn car's needed cleanin' for a long time," Bob slurred. "Think I'll get it done now."

With that, he began to sort clothes, garbage and any item in his vicinity and put them in piles. Shortly, he opened a window to throw away the garbage, in his state he cared little about littering the highway.

Next morning the two friends met for breakfast.

"Guess I did 'er last night," Bob noted. "I don't remember everything."

"Funny thing though," he went on. "The back of my car's full of garbage and I can't find my clothes."

"Don't you remember cleaning your car? Ben asked.

"Nope!" was the only reply.

"Well you did," Ben continued, "and then you threw the garbage out the window.

"Damn," said Bob, "Wrong pile."

Lorriane Fee

I Sarah wanted a date, she had to take her training seriously.

Courting Miss Sarah

The courtship was simple. Sarah lived with her family and Fred would pick up his lady in a buggy drawn by a team of horses at her father's house and go for a ride in the country. Living in the country already, a long trip was not needed.

The problem was, Fred's team was always spirited and detested standing still. Therefore, upon his arrival, he made circles around the farm house with the team and buggy until his lady love made her appearance. Much against their will, the horses would manage to chomp at the bit but remain stationary long enough for Sarah to mount the buggy.

Winters were long and often, boring so Fred would journey to the city to stay with his older sister. True, he managed to stay somewhat busy by boxing at the gymnasium, but he was growing older, and tying the knot and having a family, were crossing his mind regularly.

It was Sarah who was on his mind as he had known her since elementary school. True, there were other ladies who had their eye on him, but he knew what he wanted. What he wanted, was Sarah.

On a cold January day, Fred was once again spending the winter with his older sister. Sarah was visiting, which was much to his liking. He was comfortable, and relaxed, although a bit bored and looking for something to do.

Looking over at Sarah, Fred spoke.

"What do you think kid?" he asked, "Do you want to get married?"

Marriage was certainly Sarah's intent, although the question caught her a bit off guard. She agreed, asking only one question, "When?"

"Well," said Fred, "I think today would be a good day. What do you think?"

With the couple in full agreement, they donned their coats and headed off to find a church and a preacher. Being early in the day, a Wednesday, this task should not prove difficult. The preacher would be near his church office and they had assistance from Fred's sister. She directed the couple to a minister and they were on their way.

Making their way to the preacher's house and knocking on his door, Fred quickly explained the couple's needs.

"We'd like to get married today," was all he said.

The minister looked at the couple, both in their twenties and enquired, "Do you have a marriage license?"

"No!" the young couple admitted.

"Do you have any witnesses?" the minister went on.

Again the couple repeated their answer, "No," and asked, "Why do we need witnesses?"

"You have to have a marriage license and witnesses," they were told.

The minister went on, "Never mind. I'll make arrangements."

With that, he turned and picked up the phone to make some necessary calls. The license arrangements were made and he called a neighboring couple to witness the ceremony.

Fred and Sarah were married that day, as planned, with the only people at the wedding being the minister, his wife and a pair of strangers they had never met.

Lorriane Fee

He merely wanted to ride the waves.
Death wasn't in his plan.

Sink or Swim

Each day, is a learning experience. Indeed, some of the best lessons are learned in the School of Hard Knocks not a formal classroom.

Such was the case for Ben and Kim as they traveled during their summer break as teachers. For ten months of the year, they spent their time in classrooms in an attempt to educate children, but both were well aware of the fact that there was often more to be learned in the two remaining months. In those months, they could be themselves and not worry about setting any examples for young minds.

During this particular summer, the depth of education acquired by the pair in general and by Ben in particular, proved to be beyond their expectations. Ben learned to water ski, to drive a boat and even dove into the water of a lake and told a boat driver "I'll see you on shore." He had expected that the boat would follow him but, as his head broke water after his dive, he heard a boat motor break into full throttle and watched his ride disappearing quickly over the waves, leaving him alone in the middle of the lake. There was nothing left but Ben, the boat's wake and a far-off shore. He'd have to make his best swim ever.

He thought he would drown. He knew he was not in top physical condition and the beach was a long way off. However, he had no recourse but to begin his swim. At least they wouldn't have to drag the middle of the lake.

Far short of the beach, he ran out of energy and his breath was coming in gasps. He grabbed a floating barrel marking the swimming boundary and hung on. Fortunately, two teenage girls floated by on air mattresses, intent on enjoying the sunshine. Ben grasped at straws.

"Ladies," he said. "I've just come a long ways and I'm not sure I'll make the shore. Would you please follow me in to make sure I'm safe?"

The pair agreed, and spurred on by the new found security, the swim seemed much shorter with a young lady and an air mattress on each side of him, although he staggered from exhaustion upon trying to stand on the beach.

Ben's second lesson also fell into the area of water safety. He and Kim had purchased a knee board, intent on riding it behind the boat. They had been keen observers as others had enjoyed themselves upon the flimsy craft. They could do this.

All went well until they attempted deep water starts. They simply could not manage to get the board to hydro-plane or gain the proper stance. The answer seemed to be starting from the beach.

Ben's first attempt, with his knees strapped on to the board, saw the boat motor cough and the tip of the board go down. He was on a private journey to the bottom of the lake, sand forming the board's wake as it headed downward. Ben was mesmerized. He hung on to the ski rope and watched as fish swan quietly by. Not until the strapping on his knees tore loose did he finally pop to the surface, ski rope still held firmly in his hands.

While in the deep, he made a decision. He never wanted to come up. It was time to take scuba diving lessons.

The major lesson of the summer for the pair proved to be one of reading intent when dealing with strangers. Wanting a change of scene, it was decided to spend time in a local tavern where dancing was the call of the day.

Entering the establishment, the only seating available was on stools at the bar. The duo chose their seats and prepared to relax. But their interest was captured by a lone stranger seated close by. He brought to mind an old song they both loved, "He's an old hippie and don't know what to do."

There he sat. He was the old hippie out of the song beyond doubt. Reaching in his pocket, the hippie pulled out a roll of bills the size of which the pair had never before seen. He ordered a round of drinks for the bar and laid down a hundred dollar bill.

When the drinks appeared, they were in small, shooter, glasses and Ben didn't like the look of the prize delivered by his new found friend one bit.

"What is it?" asked Kim.

"It's Jack Daniels," Ben replied. "I can't drink it. I was sick on it when I was a kid. One taste and up it comes."

Turning to the old hippie, Ben attempted to explain his dilemma.

"Thank you very much," he said, "but I can't drink this."

Blurry eyes stared at him from across the bar for a moment, as the old hippie calmly butted a lit cigarette on the palm of his hand and said, "What?"

That was enough for Ben. He looked around for the nearest door and was pleased to discover it was right behind him. With all the will he could muster, he raised the glass, downed its contents and headed for the door to rid himself of the noxious liquid.

Among other things, the pair learned that they may be in control in their classrooms but the real world doesn't always work that way. There are times one must swallow their pride, or drink, along with whatever else life may offer, simply in search of safety.

The Bear Facts

Timmy was a good little soldier. He was well disciplined and a credit to his unit. He had gone through basic training and learned well. He proved to be responsive to instruction and well thought of by his fellow soldiers. In fact, he had become the regimental pet, a mascot so to speak.

However, Timmy had one major flaw. He was addicted to ice cream. To him, it was the most beautiful thing in the world. He would do anything to obtain the magic, decadent treat.

It seemed that everyone in camp out-ranked him. Regardless of whom Timmy would have dealings with, they would be giving the orders and he was resigned to follow them without question. Following orders is all part of day to day life on an army base anyway. It just didn't seem fair that he was to follow instructions, never having the opportunity to issue any orders but doing his duty. Perhaps it was his personality. Timmy was the quietest of the entire unit and never spoke a word edgewise, although he sometimes growled when he was tired of orders. Normally, he just listened and responded.

Eventually, Timmy had his fill of orders and instructions. What he did not have was his fill of ice cream, however. With little recourse, he determined to adjust the situation and went AWOL from his unit.

Search as they would, the soldiers could not find Timmy and his location and his return to base had become a priority. Only Fred had an idea. He felt he had the puzzle's answer. Timmy was probably hiding out in the local ice cream parlor.

Making the short journey to the parlor, Fred opened the front door and entered. He had been correct in his assumption. There sat Timmy on top of the counter, helping himself to all the ice cream he could find, none of which he had bothered to pay for. The proprietor was running to and fro in a panic. Timmy was far too big for him to handle, weighing over four hundred pounds, and he was eating him out of business. The proprietor had called the police to arrest the culprit.

Closely behind Fred, two officers appeared, guns drawn. They would take care of the menace and the threat to the owner.

Upon seeing the perpetrator of the crime, their mouths dropped open, their guns hung loosely by their sides and they simply stared. They had no idea what to do. Dealing with this giant was not included in their training.

"I'll take care of it," said Fred, much to the relief of all concerned.

He walked over to Timmy and said, "C'mon Timmy. Let's go."

Being used to following instruction and knowing Fred well, Timmy gave no argument. He climbed off the counter and followed his friend through the door and back to camp. He was well trained and a good soldier after all and would suffer no repercussions or disciplinary action.

He was the local mascot and Fred was extremely good at handling these situations, especially when it came to handling animals. And bears, such as Timmy, were his specialty.

Lorriane Fee

For Fred, the warning came in time.

The Boxer

It was to be a charity affair, just a little entertainment to raise money for the community. He was assured of that.

Members of the community grabbed onto the idea of a boxing match and approached Fred to take part, the political approach was the best.

"C'mon Fred, you were a boxer. You can do this for the community. Besides, it's only going to be a sparing match, a show, and nobody gets hurt."

It was true. Fred had been a boxer before marrying and moving to a farm to try his hand at tilling the soil. But years had passed since he had last donned boxing gloves. Then again it was for the community;

"Who's the opponent?" Fred inquired.

"Oh nobody special," he was assured. "Just some amateur we'll bring up from the city."

Fred agreed. He'd fight, but only for charity.

Little did he know his brother-in-law, Clancy, had become involved in the fundraiser. He would acquire the services of a second boxer and according to plan, find someone willing to spar for charity. Visiting a boxing club in the city, he found little problem locating just what he wanted, a seasoned and highly ranked professional.

Without hesitation, the pro agreed to take on the task, after being assured he would be paid from proceeds. That was only half the carrot offered. If he could knock Fred out, in front of the entire community, he'd receive another hundred dollars as a bonus. It was easy money for a few minutes of work.

Chuckling at his deal, Clancy, returned to assure his committee the deal was made. He had found a boxer willing to spar a few rounds with a local boy and the cost of his appearance would be minimal, practically nothing. His boxer would arrive three days before the bout and was made aware that it was only to be a sparring match. Assurance was given to Fred and the boxer's name made public. Fred recognized the boxer by name but was assured it would only help to draw a large crowd, having a professional. It would help gain proceeds and it was for a good cause.

Clancy was proud of himself. He too would make a little money with bets and he'd have the pleasure of watching Fred hit the canvas. However, to keep a secret was not one of his strong points. Clancy began to talk, he thought in confidence, to a select number of his friends in the community. He wanted to share his 'joke' with others.

News travels fast in a small community. Days before the bout, a second brother-in-law visited Fred. Wilson had heard the rumors. He would not let Fred be made a fool or be set up to get injured. He had come across the information no one was supposed to know.

"Fred, it's a set-up," he said. "They've hired the pro and offered him a hundred bucks to knock you out. It's serious, not sparring. Maybe you should think this over. Withdraw from the match."

Fred was undaunted. He may have hit the canvass had he gone into the ring unprepared but now there was a message to be sent. He'd be prepared for the onslaught and, confident as always, felt he could handle the attack. He was not the type to back away from a challenge or to experience fear. When it came right down to it, he was confident in his ability, which may have aided in Clancy's rouse.

The arrival of the professional in the community brought excitement as it signaled the approach of the fight. McLellan moved right in to a local household, making himself perfectly at home. The boxer was fed royally and decided he was on vacation. His hosts noted his lack of training going into the match.

"Shouldn't you be training?" he was asked.

"No worry" answered McLellan. "I can handle this kid easily. I don't need any training or conditioning, just a good diet. Clancy better have his money ready. This one will be over at the start. I'm already in the win column."

He may not have been on a good diet but he did eat anything he laid eyes on and partied his way to fight day. Eating, drinking and chatting up the local ladies ranked high for the professional from the city.

On the prescribed date, the two boxers took the makeshift ring in the community hall and introductions were made. While Fred mentally prepared himself, his opponent smiled with confidence and waived to the onlookers. For a hundred dollars, they'd get their show.

The opening bell proved the beginning of the end. Rather than spar, it was obvious the two were taking the event seriously. The visitor realized Fred was aware of what was supposed to happen and not about to stand for any foolishness. Blows landed hard and often from both fighters as bruises and cuts were inflicted. With the final bell, Fred was the obvious winner and a very bruised and battered professional was taken back to his host's house.

Fred had not emerged unscathed but was quite mobile on his own. His speed and defense had been the advantage needed. And he was fully conscious.

Entering the front door of his home, he was greeted by his wife who viewed his countenance with shock.

"Look at you," she said. "You're beat up something awful."

"That's ok," her husband answered. "You should see the other guy!"

Next morning dawned with proof of the winner being clear. Fred was enjoying breakfast, readying himself for a day's work in the fields. Meanwhile, the import was lying in his bed, unable to rise and dress.

His host entered the room with porridge.

"What's the matter with you?" he asked. "I thought you said that kid would be no problem."

With a chuckle he withdrew.

McLellan was silent. Days later, when his wounds had healed, the boxer disappeared.

Sleepy Mechanic

All Ben wanted to do was see a new area, to travel. His very soul burned for travel. His one previous attempt to hit the road had been derailed by an auto accident. This time, there would be no mistakes. He would finally travel.

But the best laid plans have a way of going astray. This was to turn into the adventure of a life time.

Upon his departure, he had absolutely no idea of the road to take but, with map in hand and a final destination of Las Vegas, he felt prepared. The early going proved quite routine, but the desert of Nevada waited. Traveling through the mountains was not new to him. The curves in the road presented no problem. He'd never set eyes on the desert and had no idea what was there. From reading, he knew it was hot and dry, nothing more.

Having finally reached the age of twenty one and a friend to visit in Las Vegas, he felt the excursion was a coming of age. It was his first major trip anywhere, let alone doing it alone, and he had fifteen hundred miles to cover in the old fifty seven Oldsmobile. Mechanically, he was certain the car was sound and, knowing there was no daylight speed limit on the desert highway, he could turn the car's horses loose and make good time. A hundred miles an hour sounded just fine. The old car seemed to thrive on speed and speed would certainly cut down the hours needed to reach his destination.

He followed his map faithfully and felt comfortable with his decisions until he sighted a sign welcoming him to Reno. He wasn't headed for Reno. In fact it was far off on another road according to his map reading. But here he was, and it was close to nightfall.

Pulling in for fuel at a service station, he asked directions to a motel. They were readily supplied, the service station owner also owning a place where he could lay his weary head.

Early the next morning, he was off for Vegas, some five hundred miles south as he read the map. He'd be there in six hours or less and there was no misreading his map this time.

Fifty miles into the desert, the car's engine began to misfire and eventually stopped completely. As it cooled, it would restart and give Ben a few more miles before killing. The fuel pump was shot; fuel was vaporizing in the heat of the desert and never reaching the cylinders.

Again the engine died. Ben was more than concerned this time. There was no chance to get out of the car and raise the hood. Cooling the engine would take longer. As fate would have it, he had chosen the early spring for his adventure and the car chose to die on a low spot in the desert, right where thousands of rattle snakes were making their annual migration. To emerge from the safety of his vehicle was certain to bring him harm.

For an hour, he watched the highway move around him. At last, the engine coughed, fired. The car moved ahead, a squishing sound beneath its wheels. Once again he felt safe and urged the car on. The faster he could travel, the longer the engine stayed cool, but getting over fifty miles an hour took great effort as he feathered the accelerator pedal, and to cool the fuel, he had to be over eighty five.

Some hundred miles later, he topped a rise and, much to his relief, came upon a service station. There in the shade of a hot noon day sun, sat two men, sitting on rickety chairs and leaning back against the wall of the building.

"Anybody work here?" Ben asked.

"Yep," replied the elder of the two, "He does," and motioned at his partner.

"Aren't you afraid the boss will come along and see you just sitting here?" he asked the designated worker.

Again the older man replied, "I'm the boss," he said. "She's hot t'day son, too hot fer werkin'. An' I wouln't speck him to do nothin' I wouln't do."

"Got a fuel pump problem," Ben informed the pair. "How long to get it fixed."

"Shouln' be too bad," the boss told him. "Should have one here on the bus from Vegas by mornin'"

Ben looked around. There was nothing in the area but a service station and two houses. Where he would spend the night was anyone's guess. But he remembered the snakes and was not about to venture off without a reliable mode of transportation. He'd be hungry, but at least he could sleep in his car.

The boss seemed to read his mind.

"Don't be worryin', son, you can stay the night with me and the misses," he offered.

Stay he did. Fed a hearty supper and hot breakfast, not to mention a good night's sleep and he felt better. With the car repaired, a good day had dawned.

Walking across the highway to the service station, he was overjoyed to discover his vehicle ready.

"Thanks, how much do I owe you," he asked.

"Twenty two fifty fer the fuel pump includin' labor," came the reply.

"And how much for the food and bed?" Ben asked.

"Nothin'" the owner assured him. "Son, thet fuel pump is business, it's twenty two fifty. The food and room was hospitality. They ain't no price fer thet."

It was a valuable lesson, Ben thought. One can learn a great deal from their elders if they keep their ears and eyes open. He thanked the service station attendant and crawled behind the wheel once more.

Confidence is a fleeting thing. Ben's was smashed less than fifty miles down the road. Once again, the engine died and he found himself sitting alone in the middle of nowhere. As far as he could see, nothing but desert stretched away in any direction except where it was broken slightly by the Sierra Nevada Mountains far off in the distance.

To add to Ben's concern, the one thing that was missing on this highway was traffic. There simply wasn't any.

"Here we go again," he thought aloud as he opened the car's hood. "It still doesn't run when it's hot."

Off in the distance, he heard the most pleasant of sounds. A motor hummed and was getting closer. Within moments a semi topped a rise. It was coming toward him. Perhaps he could flag it down and catch a ride for help. He was disgusted enough with his car, it could rot in the desert for all he cared.

Flagging the semi down proved unnecessary. Spotting the car and stranded driver, the eighteen-wheeler pulled to a stop behind him and the driver emerged.

"Fuel pump?" was the simple question Ben heard.

"Yeah," he replied. "I had trouble yesterday, had it changed and it still doesn't work."

"Not surprising," observed the trucker. "Lots of mechanical pumps give trouble in the desert. Next time put on an electric one. I can fix your problem."

Ben was elated, a mechanical truck driver with tools. His confidence was returning in leaps and bounds as he watched the driver return to the cab of his truck.

But it wasn't tools the driver dug from beneath the seat of his tractor. Instead, he handed Ben a small box.

"Here," he said. "I'd never be without a box of these. Put them on your gas line between the pump and the carb and you'll be fine."

Ben did as instructed but his mind was filled with doubt. A new fuel pump merely extended his misery and now this trucker was going to fix his problem with a mere box of wooden clothes pins. It had to work or he'd be standing in the desert looking for a clothes line for his pins. The eighteen-wheeler was already pulling away, leaving him alone with his problem. Again his confidence sagged.

Ben felt stupid, standing in the hot desert putting wooden pins on his gas line. What else could he do? He was promised it would fix the problem and why else would the driver take the time to stop? Just to make a joke of him?

Fix it, it did. Through the remainder of his trip, the car rolled over the pavement smoothly, the engine never missing a beat.

"That's it," Ben thought. "Heck with tools. From now on, I leave the wrenches alone and carry clothes pins."

As he pulled into Las Vegas, Ben was still thinking about his excursion. He was pleased with himself for having over come the difficulties of the trip. But he couldn't help but wonder why the mechanic hadn't known of the clothes pin trick. Ben decided the mechanic merely lived in the desert while the trucker traveled it.

Life Savers

Lifesavers! The little round candy with the hole in the middle is what we think of immediately. As children, we loved them. They came in so many flavors. Or a Life Saver could also be the life guard at the beach. Picture them! Brawny skinned, muscular men or vivacious women would 'fit the bill'.

But Ben's Life Saver was far different. He wasn't handsome. He wasn't tanned, He wasn't brawny. In fact, he was a grizzled old man, serving gas in the small city of Missoula, Montana. Sweet, however, he was. He was a true diplomat in all respects.

Leaving Las Vegas early in the morning, Ben was on the road heading for Canada. He was far too upset to admit to his hosts that he had experienced a minor accident while sleeping, so he arose early, and headed off on the next leg of his journey. He had been welcomed with open arms upon his arrival, but such would not be the case when the damage he had created was noticed. He had to leave, and leave he did. It seemed the best strategy under the circumstances. He'd just left a note of apology and left.

Thanks to a car that enjoyed being driven at one hundred miles an hour and the absence of speed limits in Nevada and during the daytime in Montana, he was certain he could reach his destination without sleep, in spite of it being a journey of fifteen hundred miles. But as time fleeted, he began to question his theory. Had all gone according to plan, perhaps? He was wrong.

The day began well, but a few hundred miles out of Vegas and into the desert where only the desert hares dared to live, disaster struck. Looking down at his gauges, he noticed a light flickering on the dashboard. He was out of oil in his engine if the red light was to be believed. He would take no chances with this sort of warning - not in the desert anyway.

Ben coasted to a stop, turned off his engine and emerged from the vehicle to check on the oil problem. The dipstick in his engine confirmed his worst fears. It was dry. Again, he tested. There must be a mistake. Again, the dipstick came up dry. How could that be? His car was not an oil burner, yet there was no oil to be measured.

Fortunately, Ben had the foresight to plan for just such an emergency. He carried three cans of oil in the trunk. He put one can into the engine and checked the oil level. Again, the dipstick was dry. Only after three cans did he finally see oil on the dipstick. This would be enough to get him to a service station, but where had the oil gone? He knew his engine was, or at least had been— till now, in good operating condition.

He slid under the car, his back to the hot sand and surveyed the situation. There was a large gap between the oil pan and the engine. The gasket had shrunk in the heat of the desert and the oil splashed out. It was obvious from the condition of the car's undercarriage.

Having no wrenches to make the necessary repairs, the best he could do was lift the oil pan with his knees and tighten the screws which held it in place with his fingers. Several frustrating minutes passed, which seemed more like hours. He managed to get each bolt finger-tight. That would last him until he finally found a service station if he drove slowly.

Twenty miles along a lonely road, in the town of Winnamucha, he had his first success of the day. A mechanic loaned him wrenches and he purchased enough oil to bring the level up to normal. He was on the road.

Looking at his map, Ben searched for the shortest route to his destination. Unfortunately, he was young and a poor map reader. He chose a road that appeared to be short, but ignored the twists the map showed. He chose the Snake River Canyon route and was soon to learn how it got its name. It was, indeed, exactly like a snake, following the Snake River and slowing his progress beyond belief. With night fall, his journey slowed even more. He was now more than twelve hours into a drive he had felt would be complete in eighteen hours and far from his destination. Fatigue began to set in.

On each straight section of road, and there were few, Ben's head drooped forward and his eyes closed. He was about to fall asleep and plunge into the Snake River. His only life saver was the white crosses which dotted each turn. On sight of them, his eyes opened wide. Someone had died here and he didn't plan to join them. Obviously, it was a dangerous course he had chosen, as the white crosses dotted the entire roadside.

An eternity passed before Ben found his way out of the canyon and onto straight road. His fuel gauge was showing the need for a service station. At last, lights appeared on the horizon. He was approaching a town. He would have the availability of fuel and continue his drive. He wanted to reach the Canadian border, by the time the crossing opened at Sweet Grass, in the morning.

The car seemed to be driving itself, with a zombie behind the wheel. All thought had left Ben. He was merely a robot who traveled wherever the machine attempted to take him. Eighteen hours had passed since he departed Las Vegas and both time and miles, not to mention his automotive problems, were taking their toll. The automobile chose the first service station and pulled to the pumps.

Ben sat there, stationary in his car, and waited.

Eons later, an elderly gentleman, working the graveyard shift made his way to the car window.

"Fill 'er up," he asked.

Ben merely nodded.

"Where you bin drivin' from?" he went on.

Ben admitted he had had a long drive. He told the gentleman he had left Vegas that morning and had been held up with car problems but now was here and heading for the border by the time it opened in the morning.

Much to Ben's surprise, the elderly one finished filling the car with gas and opened the driver's door.

"Slide over," was all he said.

Ben, the zombie, did as instructed.

The life saver slid under the steering wheel, backed the car across the service station lot to a darker location, took the keys from the ignition and looked at Ben.

"I see you have a sleeping bag in the back seat," he said. "I'm going to take your keys, you slide into that bag and sleep for an hour. I'll wake you."

Ben was far too tired to argue. He merely shook his head in agreement and crawled into the sleeping bag. Folding his arm under his head, he lay down, closed his eyes and was immediately asleep.

He was certain he had merely closed his eyes when the knocking came at his window.

"Here's your keys," said the life saver. "I came back in an hour and checked, but you were sleeping pretty heavy so I didn't call you. You've been asleep two hours, but you'll still make that border when it opens."

Shaking the cobwebs out his brain, Ben made his way to the driver's seat and was handed his keys.

"Now you drive careful, you hear," said the old timer, turning his back and disappearing into the service station.

Ben was on the road. But there was no more nodding off, there was straight road, and no more white crosses to shake him awake. He was on his own on a perfect road, heading north.

True to the old timer's prediction, Ben reached the border crossing and pulled his car to a stop just as a border guard came to man the booth.

The questions were short and Ben was over and on his way. But he had regrets.

He knew the elderly man at the service station had been a Life Saver. Ben had been far too tired to make a sensible decision and beyond driving farther. But he would have tried. He knew he would have gone on had the gentleman not taken charge. What bothered him most, however, was that he could never thank his guardian angel and didn't even know his name.

Yes, Life Savers may be tasty with holes in the middle or gorgeous beach dwellers, but Ben's had been aged, gnarled and not at all attractive. Beneath the surface, sweet he may have been. He was most certainly caring.

Ben had learned a valuable lesson. He realized the one way he could thank his benefactor was to be caring and help protect others. Sometimes, the most important lessons in life are taught by the most unexpected people.

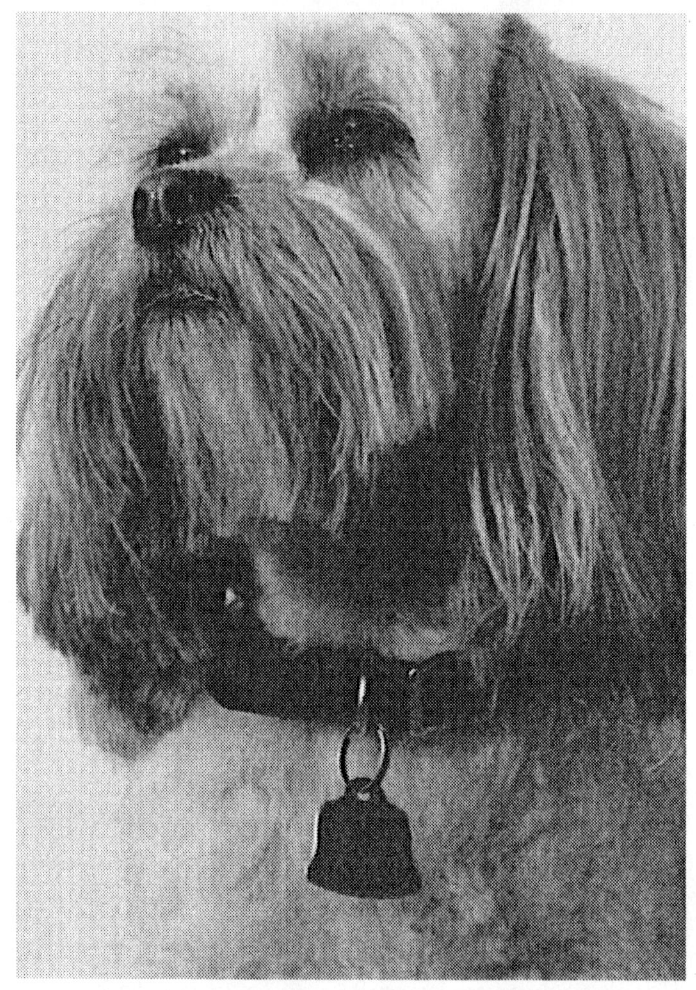

With the attitude of a queen, she took over the house in short order.

Mocha Mo

He wanted a dog, his mind was made up. Not just any dog would do. It had to be a Lhasa Apso. During a depressing period of his life, a friend's Lhasa had done a great deal to pull him through. Now the search was on.

Prior to making up his mind to acquire a dog, there had been many ads in the paper but now they were completely absent. He checked the pet column daily in search of his dog.

An ad appeared. "Female Lhasa Apso for sale," it read.

"There's my dog," Ben told himself and made the call.

Being told the dog was eight months old and with its second owner, questions arose.

"Why are you trying to sell her?" he asked.

"Coyotes," was the reply. "There's lots of coyotes around here and we're afraid they may get her."

Ben agreed to see the dog. It was a long drive, but it was also the only dog available. He knew he shouldn't go to pick up a single dog. He should find a variety of puppies and let the dog choose him.

Upon arriving he noticed an eight foot high fence. He again felt something strange but decided to check it out.

When the door to the house was opened a pretty little female Lhasa made a fuss over him but ignored her current owners. It was love at first sight. They were a match.

The dog paid for, Ben was questioned. He wasn't surprised at being questioned as any caring dog owner would want to ensure the animal had a good home. But these questions and cautions were different.

"You better take her bed with you," the lady of the house instructed.

Ben couldn't see how his living conditions would allow this and expressed his concerns.

"Well," asked the lady, "then where will she sleep."

"On my bed," he replied.

The lady became extremely indignant. "She's not allowed on furniture," Ben was informed.

He was tiring of the attitudes he saw around him. "Ma'am," he replied, "You're holding my money. Now she's allowed on furniture."

Her former owner picked up a leash. "She's pretty good on a leash," he said, "If you can catch her."

The dog ran.

"May I try that," asked Ben. "What's her name?"

Before even learning the dog's name, Mocha, for that was it, ran to him, stopped and waited for him to put on the leash. With that, dog and new owner calmly walked out the door.

They were yet to be free of warnings. "If she lies in her bed or in a corner," the former owner told Ben, "don't touch her. She's tired."

Ben opened the car door as he heard someone say, "You'll have to lift her. She can't jump in there."

He was wrong. Mocha bailed into the car, curled up on the passenger seat and proceeded to go to sleep. She was going home and she knew it.

Lorriane Fee

Except for his shaking, Wayne stood motionless in the doorway, waiting for his mother's voice to shatter the darkness.

Long Road Home

Depending on your approach, the shortest route may turn out to be the longest. Such is the case, particularly, when the road leads home and that isn't exactly where one would care to be at the moment or under an existing situation.

This was the case with Wayne.

The high school party had ended and Wayne was wandering along the road on his way home, walking three times the distance required as he staggered from one ditch to the other. Fortunately for Wayne, two friends, who had not been at the party, happened to come along.

"What's with you?" they asked.

"Well," Wayne drawled as well as he could in his condition, slurring every word "I kind of overdid it. Now I gotta walk it off before I get home. Mom's gonna kill me if she ever sees me like this. I have to be sober when I get home and I gotta make curfew."

His friends were in full agreement. They were familiar with Wayne's mother and knew he would pay for his behavior. He was underage. He was drunk. And he was going to be in big trouble. His weekend could very well have come to an abrupt end when he entered his own front door.

"C'mon," his friends said. "Get in the car. We'll go somewhere and walk it off."

Heading for a country road out of sight of anyone, his friends, Ben and Larry were determined to help him. If he was going to make it home on time, he had to change his condition and do it rapidly. There was no time to waste.

Stopping a few miles out of town, the pair managed to pry their drunken friend from the car, onto a gravel road. A walk in the fresh spring air would get him going in no time and they could take him home. It didn't.

A few gulps of fresh air and Wayne's condition worsened.

"Ya gotta help," they heard his slurred words report. "Can't walk."

It was the understatement of the day. Each time Wayne attempted to take a step, he fell to his knees on the gravel road. Each fall, he pulled himself erect without complaint and readied for the next trip.

With Ben on one side, Larry on the other and Wayne's arms across their shoulders, the trio began to hike up and down the road in a valiant attempt to return their friend to a sober state. But something was wrong. Wayne stood six feet six inches tall, the pair was only five foot six, yet all three heads were at the same level as they walked along.

Looking down, Ben made a startling discovery. Wayne was walking through the gravel on his knees.

"Hey!" he gasped. "doesn't that hurt?"

"What hurt?" came the reply.

Wayne was in such a condition, he hadn't even noticed.

An hour passed but the condition of the giant failed to improve. Instead, his humor was changing. Everything was hilarious and he laughed constantly.

"Look guys," he said, "rocks, pretty rocks," as he looked at the gravel under his knees. "And there's a whole bunch of lights in the sky, and three moons, and...... wow."

Larry and Ben had about all they could take of this moonlight stroll. Their efforts were of no help as the alcohol Wayne had consumed earlier continued to build in his blood and rush to his brain. He was, to say the least, thoroughly pickled.

"That's it," Larry blurted in frustration. "We can't spend all night doing this. Let's just take him home. He got this way. He can work it out with his Mom."

Ben agreed but had his reservations.

"If we take him home like this," he said, "we may never see him again. His Mom will lock him up for a long, long time. We should give it just a little more time."

Time did the opposite of help. Wayne's condition continued to worsen. In the end, Larry's wish was granted. Wayne was going home.

'Home' they went. However, neither Ben nor Larry wanted any part of meeting an angry mother. They unloaded their buddy, opened the screen door and propped him up against the door jam. Finding a house key in Wayne's jacket pocket, they unlocked the front door, pushed their friend inside, shut the door and left.

Much to the surprise of Ben and Larry, they met their friend in the local coffee shop the very next morning. They were certain he would be grounded, if not imprisoned on a life sentence but there he was, a slight headache his main complaint.

"How'd ya make out?" Larry asked.

"Pretty good," was Wayne's reply. "I was standin' inside the door and Mom called and asked if it was me. I walked right up to her bedroom, sat on the bed and said, 'Mom, I'm drunk.' I guess she didn't believe me. All she said was 'Wayne, go to bed!' and said nothin' this morning."

"She was kind of wondering though. How'd I get holes in the knees of my pants?"

There the lesson was learned by the three high school boys; always be honest with your parents. It's the best policy.

And who knows? If you're very, *very* lucky, they may not believe you.

Kill 'Em with Kindness

School was out for the Christmas break, teachers and students were relaxed and looking forward to Santa's big day and the sun was shining. The roads were dry with only small patches of snow lying here and there in the fields. How could life get better than this?

He cruised along, inhaled deeply and allowed his breath to escape slowly. The holiday season was wonderful. Everyone, even the shoppers in the busy malls seemed to be smiling and wishing complete strangers the best of the season.

"Why," he wondered, "couldn't it be like this throughout the year?"

Glancing in his rear view mirror, he noticed a car rapidly catching him. Perhaps he was going far too slow. He glanced at the speedometer. No, he was actually going ten miles per hour over the speed limit. He wouldn't be holding anyone up and felt safe from any possibility of getting a speeding ticket. Even the police were into the good will of the season and tended to look the other way as long as traffic was moving smoothly.

With only two cars on the road, traffic was certainly moving smoothly.

The car continued to gain on him until he noticed it was within feet of his rear bumper, far too close to react should he be forced to hit the brakes. This was a driver in a hurry. The aggression seemed to worry him somewhat as it continued to close the distance between vehicles, attempting to force him to a higher speed.

"No worry," he told himself. "It's a two lane road but there are lots of passing zones ahead. They'll pass right away."

Passing zone after passing zone whizzed past his wheels but he continued to be tailgated. The opportunities to pass were plentiful but the driver behind him seemed to be mesmerized by his tail lights. If he was forced to apply the breaks, he would be hit from behind and he knew it. There was no chance of stopping in a hurry on the wet roads, if the driver even had time to touch the breaks.

"Gotta be careful," he cautioned himself. "One mistake and I get in an accident, hit from the rear."

Several miles down the road, he saw the road breaking into an extra lane. Now the driver would finally pass.

Approaching a traffic light, he noticed it was about to turn red and came to a stop in the left turn lane. His tag-along friend pulled up beside him on the passenger side and came to a stop as well. He was finally free of the danger.

Glancing over, he saw a very irate lady driver who was shaking her fist in his direction and making numerous signs, including signaling for him to open his window. He complied. Did she need to talk to him? Had he made some traffic error of which he wasn't aware? Or perhaps he actually knew the driver.

Through the open window, he heard the irate lady's voice.

"How dare you hold me up," she shouted. "Don't you know I'm in a hurry? I have a lot of things to do."

His first reaction was shock. Then he regained his thought processes and prepared to reply. He was determined to be nice. He would set an example and show his Christmas spirit. He would make a point by being nice.

"I'm terribly sorry," he said. "I really didn't realize you were in a hurry or I could have pulled into a driveway to let you pass. It was, indeed, very thoughtless of me to only drive ten miles an hour over the speed limit when you were in such a hurry. Would it have helped if I'd stopped on the side of the road?"

The lady was taken back by his calm sincerity. She could barely believe her ears but did get the message he was trying to send. His meaning and his words differed greatly. His sarcasm had shown through.

"Well," she blurted, agitation remaining on the edge of her voice. "There's only two days until Christmas you know and I have shopping to do. I've barely begun with gifts for the family and I haven't even bought a turkey yet."

"I truly am sorry," he reiterated. "I had no intention of keeping you from such important business."

"And that's another thing," he added. "It's so hard to plan for Christmas when they keep changing the date every year. Wouldn't you agree?"

With an audible gasp, the lady flipped him the third and spun around the corner, intent on her shopping. Unfortunately, she failed to notice the red light and met a new friend in the intersection.

With the third finger still prominently displayed, she accelerated right into the side of a passing police cruiser. The shocked officer sat and stared at the grill of a car placed firmly in his door and a lady sitting behind the wheel, her finger held high in salute. Was it for him?

"Yes," he muttered aloud. "Sometimes one really can teach a lesson better by being calm."

And while the lady driver explained herself to the police officer, off he went, set to get on with his own Christmas shopping.

Three Weddings - Two Grooms

Irene was a looker. Of this there was no doubt. In fact, everywhere Irene went, heads turned to admire her beauty.

One of her favorite things was dating. And she had no shortage of dates. The young men seemed to line up for her attention.

"I am the fox," she thought. "Let the hounds take up the chase."

She loved to be seen in fast cars with fancy dates. She loved to dance and she loved romance. Over all, she was in her glory in dating circles.

But all good things must come to an end. The day finally came when she met Jim. Jim was tall, handsome and wore his army uniform everywhere. He was a stunning figure of a man. How could a girl discourage the affections of a soldier? He did look handsome in that uniform.

Jim and Irene became a steady couple. Where one was seen, both were seen. They enjoyed each other's company, dancing, movies and just plain snuggling together in Jim's car.

One night the quiet Jim finally summoned enough courage to approach a topic which had been foremost on his mind for some time now. He had been waiting a long time for the proper moment and it was time to pop the question.

"Irene," he stammered, "I'll be going off to war soon. Before I go, would you marry me?"

Irene was overwhelmed by the suggestion but managed to blurt out, "Yes."

The plans were official. The date was set. The hall was booked. The church was booked. The preacher was booked. A wedding cake was baked and decorated, including the names Irene and Jim, with a pair of porcelain figures perched proudly on its top to represent the happy couple.

When the designated day dawned, happiness abounded throughout the family and before anyone knew it, they were off to the church. With the guests in place to watch the ceremony, the minister appeared. The groom and groomsmen took their places and the bridesmaids made their way up the aisle to the sound of organ music, to wait at the front of the church for the bride's appearance.

The organist, on cue, broke into "Here Comes the Bride".

But she didn't. The doors at the back of the church failed to open as the guests, groomsmen and bridesmaids awaited the bride's arrival with great expectations. Behind those doors, there was a problem.

Irene looked up at her father and said, "Daddy, I can't do this. I'm not ready to be married."

Taking her arm, her father looked at her compassionately.

"Don't worry dear," he said. "I understand. I'll tell everyone the wedding is off."

Striding through the door to the accompaniment of "Here Comes the Bride," Big Daddy made his way up the steps to the pulpit and made his announcement, much to the surprise of all present.

"I'm sorry," he said, "but the wedding is off."

Jim dropped his head and made it to the entry of the church as the guests patted him on the back and assured him it was "all for the better."

The wedding party went home and the guests departed while questioning the entire affair. Irene went home with Big Daddy to store her wedding dress.

Jim was off to war in a foreign land he'd never seen, to fight an enemy he had nothing against and for a reason of which he was unsure. He only knew it was his turn, his duty. He'd been ordered to the war and ordered to fight, so fight he would.

Letters began shortly after his arrival in the war zone as Irene assured him that she had made a disastrous mistake and would wait for him, faithfully. She would be there upon his return. The future would be theirs.

But in war, the future could be the next moment. Jim wanted Irene to wait, but he felt she should also prepare for the worst and be able to care for herself. He assured her of this, just in case he never returned.

Irene enrolled in the women's army corps and continued to send daily letters to Jim. Life was boring. Eventually she returned to the dating scene which she found exciting. Exciting that is, until she met Floyd which brought a Dear John letter to Jim telling him of her decision. She would marry Floyd.

Floyd was the answer to every girl's dream. He appeared to have just stepped from the movie screen and had a romantic personality as well. Irene and Floyd became an inseparable duo. If you saw one, you saw both.

The romantic Floyd decided to pop the magic question. He dropped to one knee, took Irene by the hand

and asked her to be his bride as he held out a sparkling diamond ring.

How could a girl say no to such an offer? She couldn't. Irene promptly accepted.

Soon the plans were official. The date was set. The hall was booked. The church was booked. The preacher was booked. A wedding cake was baked and decorated, including the names Irene and Floyd with a pair of porcelain figures placed neatly on top to represent the happy couple.

With the arrival of the designated day, the guests were in place, the groom and groomsmen were in place and the minister was in place. Down the aisle came the bridesmaids as they were welcomed in to the sound of organ music. The organist broke into "Here Comes the Bride.

But she didn't.

Behind those doors, there was trouble.

Irene looked up at her father and said, "Daddy, I can't do this. I promised to wait for Jim and I still love him."

"It's all right," muttered Big Daddy as he took his daughter by the arm. "I'll take care of it."

With those words, Big Daddy trudged through the doors to the sound of Here Comes the Bride, made his way up the isle, stumbled up the steps, slumped over the pulpit and announced that the wedding was off.

The disappointed guests left. Floyd went out the back door with his groomsmen, the bridesmaids tallied up how much their gowns had cost while serving no purpose and the bride went home with Big Daddy to store her wedding dress alongside the first.

The letters to Jim resumed with Irene telling of her undying love and how she couldn't wait until he got home so they could be married. Each one ended with a caution to be careful just before the word love.

When Jim returned, Irene was waiting to meet him at the station. He was her true love and she knew it. It took a little to get used to the new Jim though, as war had changed him, but she was undaunted in her efforts. This was the man she would marry.

The plans were official. The date was set. The hall was booked. The church was booked. The preacher was booked. A stale wedding cake was recycled from the first wedding, including the names Irene and Jim complete with a pair of porcelain figures on top representing the happy couple.

On the designated day, the guests were in their places, the minister took his place behind the pulpit, the groom and groomsmen waited at the front of the church. The bridesmaids made their way down the aisle accompanied by organ music and everyone awaited the arrival of the bride. The honored guests were filled with caution. There were no expectations on their part.

The organist broke into, "Here Comes the Bride", and the eyes of the invited guests turned to the rear of the church.

But she didn't.

Jim thought, "Here we go again."

Behind those doors there was a problem. Irene looked up at her father and said, "Daddy, I can't go through with this."

Big Daddy looked down at his daughter, took her by the arm and said, "The Hell you can't," as he promptly dragged her through the doors and down the aisle.

When the preacher asked, "Who gives this bride to this man?" he was cut off by Big Daddy blurting, "I do!"

Irene's "I do's" were loud and clear with her father standing behind her.

Jim, however, had knees shaking like branches blowing in a strong wind, as he wondered if the bride would stay through the entire ceremony until the knot was tied or bolt for the door. He was prepared for the worst.

When the party was over, the guests went home content with the outcome of the day. Big Daddy went home satisfied that he wouldn't have any more wedding bills for a while, and Jim and Irene went home, married, to live happily ever after.

Big Daddy knew best. Sixty years later and the couple remained romantic and in love.

The Earache

Timmy had the earache. It went on day after day and kept him lying in bed with the pain. Infection of the ear was passing through the community and it was not unusual for him or anyone to be down with the pain.

A week passed while he lay on his cot, sleepless. The nights proved little better, and sleep deprivation was becoming a definite factor in his condition. Entering the weekend, nothing had changed. He lay and moaned or held his ears.

His mother had tried many remedies. First it was towels soaked in cold water. This only seemed to aggravate the situation. The more cold towels she supplied, the more Timmy held them to his ear, the worse the earache became. She attempted a second cure.

This time it was a hot water bottle, filled from the water tank on the wood stove. Timmy lay on it with one ear and then the other. The ear on the hot water seemed to improve. The other merely became more obvious to him as the pain seemed to increase. Soon more towels arrived. They too had been soaked in water, this time hot. But there was a difference. Air passed through the towels which had been blocked by the hot water bottle. The pain increased in spite of the heat.

Pulling out the old doctor book, present in nearly every farm family home at the time, the family searched for a remedy. Earache was a common malady and the answer would be there. It was.

The doctor book prescribed drops available at any drug store. A short trip to town and the drops had been secured. A few drops in each ear and the infection was sure to pass, but it may take a few days according to the book.

Timmy was happy he would be better in a few days but, in the meantime, the pain was becoming unbearable.

Saturday morning, his sister, Yvonne, arrived home from school to spend the weekend with her family. The boy idolized his big sister and her arrival was medicinal. Yvonne could do nothing wrong in his eyes. She was perfection with feet. As a little boy, learning to speak, he was taught that she was his sister. But he was incapable of saying sister and it came out as 'Diddy'. Even now, he referred to her by that name.

Diddy came upstairs to visit her little brother. She loved him in spite of him being a problem at times and wanted to help.

"Timmy," she said, "is there anything I can do?"

Timmy knew exactly what was needed. He needed to hear a pleasant voice sing to him. It would take his mind off his pain.

"Would you sing to me Diddy?" he replied.

His sister began to sing. He kept her singing throughout the weekend and the ear ache seemed to subside with each song. By the time she left to return to school, the entire episode was over and Timmy was well again, playing happily with his toys.

He hugged his sister and said goodbye for another week. She was the wonder cure beyond doubt.

He had forgotten about the ear drops. They were useless compared to Diddy's singing. She had cured him.

Years later, he heard his sister sing again. He had cause to wonder how her singing could have helped the earache. Perhaps it was the drops after all.

Lorriane Fee

She seemed to disagree with his choice of colors

Painted Into a Corner

The house was old, rickety and falling apart. Merely walking across the living room floor resulted in getting slivers between your toes if shoes weren't worn. Something had to be done to improve his living conditions.

Wanting to cover all the bases, Ben began by going over his renovation plans with his new wife. First he would sand that old floor and refinish it. The second project would be painting. If he was to become extremely energetic, he could brighten the old place up by installing a drop ceiling in the living room. With a nine foot ceiling, there was plenty of room for the plan. The final touch would be hidden lighting behind the ceiling. That was certain to make the run down shack livable.

His wife had reservations. "It's not our house," she said. "With you in school we haven't much money. Who's going to pay for all this?"

"Got that figured too," Ben replied. "I'll do the work, the landlord will pay. I'll bet on it."

Cooperation on the part of the rental company was beyond Ben's wildest dreams. Of course they would pay for any materials he needed. "Just take it off the rent," they said.

On the down side, Ben needed his own tools. They wouldn't pay rental for equipment. With a cheap electric drill, he sanded the entire living room floor, bought varnish and refinished it. The appearance was pleasing. Beneath the grey rotted wood, lay beautiful oak hardwood.

He turned his decorating efforts in the direction of the old fireplace. It was an ugly brown so Ben, now with a helper, his visiting brother-in-law Rick, decided to change the color. White brightened the room again. The old place was beginning to take shape.

The walls remained a challenge. Picking up white paint, the painting pair went to work and soon finished the walls. But now it was far too bright in the room.

"We have to add contrast," Ben noted.

His helper agreed.

Back to the hardware store they went and purchased a gallon of black paint.

"Stripes! That's what she needs Rick. Stripes," Ben advised his partner.

Stripes it was. The entire wall was painted in black and white stripes running from floor to ceiling. Creative as they were, the width of stripes varied with a wide black one right in the corner of the room.

"Great effect," said Rick. "Look at the corner. It seems to move around. You have to look right up to the ceiling to see where it really is."

Unfortunately, for the creators, the front door opened just as they were admiring their work.

"What have you done?" Ben's wife asked in horror.

"Don't you like it?" was Ben's only reply. "We're just going to do one more wall and leave the other two white."

"No! You are not," his wife said, adamant in her position. "Stop right now!"

Ben decided he would never paint again. He was a creator of class and no one appreciated his efforts. He was an 'artist'. No one else had any taste and he wouldn't waste his talent on the unappreciative.

For years, he stuck to his word. But, as fate would have it, he finally painted himself into a corner and forced the issue. Having purchased a new house, he built a deck for his wife for Mother's Day. It was a large deck and painting would be a major job.

"We'll paint it on the weekend," his wife pointed out.

"We?" replied the shocked Ben. "We? What's this 'we'? I don't paint."

He was quickly informed that he was about to begin to paint whether he liked it or not.

True to her word, when the weekend arrived, he found that his lady love had purchased *two* paint brushes. One she handed to him with instructions of where to begin painting. It would be his job to paint the railing which Ben thought was the toughest job of all. Bowing to a higher authority, he began to spread paint. But it failed to meet with the approval of the foreman. She promptly and constantly reminded him of how the procedure was to be carried out.

Ben hated painting to begin with, and he certainly hated the constant instruction. If he was going to do the job, why couldn't he do it his way? It was only a deck after all.

At last his wife said the magic words, and they weren't "I love you." What she said was, "If you can't do it right, don't do it at all!"

It was the sweetest thing Ben had ever heard her say. He had painted himself into a corner by building the deck and now he could see his way free of the project. Caught with his brush on the up stroke, he merely allowed the motion of his hand to continue. The paint brush looped over his shoulder and fell on the lawn.

Happily, he walked away, never to paint again. He did have to pick up his paint brush a week later. Someone had to take it off the lawn.

Dad's Treasure

Chris and Chris were best friends. They were inseparable from the time they met in elementary school.

It was an amazing friendship since they seemed to have little in common. Nonetheless, they managed to have enough to work out a friendship. From a very early age, they swore they would be best man at each other's wedding.

In junior high school, both boys enrolled in cooking, a class expected to be, if not reserved to, at least directed toward girls - boys took woodworking. However, when the school awards were handed out, there was a tie for top grades in the cooking class. The awards went to Chris and Chris who proudly marched to the podium to accept their awards. They did it together.

School let out for the summer and children went home early, but teachers stayed in the schools until the end of the normal school day. The pair was at wits' ends as to how to spend their time when ending grade seven. Wandering around the neighborhood, by chance, they came upon video game arcade, in which they would pass some time.

The activity lasted only a short while as the pair had limited funds. It mattered not. Chris recalled his father putting the change from his pocket into a large jar each evening. There were plenty of quarters in the jar. They would pay a visit to the jar of riches. Dad would never know if they only took a few coins. There were plenty of them for everyone to enjoy.

Passing the afternoon became an easy affair, although it did require several trips back to the jar for new funds. It was like having their own, private treasure, or perhaps finding the pot of gold at the end of the rainbow. The funds seemed endless. There must have been hundreds of dollars in that jar.

Throughout the summer, Chris' father continued to deposit his change in the jar and, on occasion, would count the coins, partly to pass the time and partly to see how his coin saving was progressing. Whenever the amount grew to a certain stage, he had promised his wife, Storm, a trip to Hawaii. But the counting was confusing. The coins in the jar seemed to be at a standstill, although Ben was certain he was putting in enough change that it should be growing.

In confusion, Chris' father grew bored of attempting to sort out the mystery. During the summer, he had less change in his pocket and simply didn't deposit any in the jar, he concluded. Rather than growing, he seemed to have fewer coins each time he counted the money.

Thinking his wife had been borrowing coins for shopping center carts, to pay the paper boy or parking meters, Chris' father did not pursue the issue of the missing coins. It simply wasn't worth worrying about. They would manage the trip to Hawaii without the coinage. It was a game for Ben anyway.

The following year Ben and his wife Storm were off to Hawaii. The finances were available and the coin jar was empty. On the flight to the Islands, Ben turned to his wife with a comment.

"With all the coins you took from my coin jar," he said, "we're lucky to be going anywhere."

Storm merely stared.

"What did you use all the coins I put in that jar for anyway?" he went on.

"What coins?" Storm finally replied. "I never took any coins from your jar. In fact I added a few of my own to help and get on this trip sooner. You said we wouldn't go until the jar was full and I wanted to go soon."

Ben shook his head in disbelief. Where had those coins been going? He couldn't come up with a single idea.

Fifteen years later, Chris was married in a beautiful ceremony to a lovely young lady. And true to their word, the second Chris was the best man.

The coin jar had been long forgotten by everyone except the best man. When he rose, walked to the microphone and began to give his speech, the mystery was solved at last.

Chris stood to make a toast to the bridesmaids, and should have perhaps stopped when his job was complete. But he couldn't satisfy himself with that. He was the only one who remembered the treasure cove and had comments. The entire mystery unraveled right before the groom's father's eyes. Ben couldn't believe his ears.

"When we got out of grade seven," the best man began, "we were playing a few video games to pass the time. But our money didn't last long. Then Chris said he knew where to find coins."

"It was a great summer," the best man went on. "His Dad had a coin jar and as fast as he could put coins in it, we took them out. Chris said we weren't doing anything wrong. His Dad had lots of coins and we were just helping out the local economy. We would have put some in but it was enough work just taking them out."

At last the mystery of the missing coins was solved.

Upper Deck

Long be the painter's life,
Who paints a deck with his wife.
Whatever he may say or do
She's sure to take a shot or two.

Be it strokes, too long,
He knows he's wrong,
Or paint too thick,
So it won't stick.

Whatever he may try to do,
He'll always face a shout or two.

Benjamin Bratt was proud of himself as he sat down to breakfast with his wife Storm. The brand new house was finished and they had moved in. Spring was in the air and he could finally get started on what promised to be a busy summer.

There were fences to build, landscaping, deck construction, and of course, painting. Now, Benjamin didn't enjoy painting. In fact he despised the work. But he was certain Storm would do most of the painting if he merely did the construction. And in a brand new neighborhood, he was certain neighbors would help each other. The year before, their lots had been a grain field.

It was Mother's Day and Benjamin spotted his new neighbor, Dave, hovering around the back yard. Dave was a great guy but somewhat different from those to which Benjamin was accustomed. Dave was from Newfoundland and marched to a different drum than did the prairie folk.

Opening the garden doors, Benjamin called out, "Whatcha doin' Dave?"

"I bin wonderin' where we'd be buildin' decks and when," came the response.

Before Benjamin could reply, his wife, Storm interjected.

"I was hoping that would be my Mother's Day present," she said. "But it is Mother's Day, so it won't happen now."

"And why not? And why not?" the Newfie asked.

"Dave," said Benjamin. "C'mon, it's Sunday and we haven't even ordered wood yet."

"Well then, we'll just have to be getting' down to the lumber yard and doin' that," was the Newfoundlander's response. "It's early. They'll 'ave it 'ere by noon."

Benjamin Bratt could not believe any of what was going on and certainly did not think lumber could be delivered the same day. But with Dave pulling and Storm shoving, he had no recourse other than to go to the lumber yard and try.

Over the past few days, he had come to know his new neighbor quite well, so he wasn't the least surprised when Dave took over as they entered the lumber yard and walked up to the lumber desk.

"Me buddy's got a list of lumber we needs," he told the clerk. "We don't care how much it costs, just get it out."

That didn't quite ring true with Benjamin, who was paying the bill, but he went along. He could check the price when the quote came. When it did, he had no time to speak before Dave broke in again.

"Now, we wants it to this address by two this afternoon," he said.

The lumber clerk was in shock. A same day delivery was out of the question.

"We can't have it there that soon, sir," he said. "We're pretty busy today and it is Mother's Day Sunday. We'll have it there by Wednesday.

"No you won't. No you won't," Dave said forcefully. "You'll 'ave 'er der by two or you can keep it."

As they were about to leave, Benjamin noticed some hallway lights.

"Hey, Dave," he said, "Aren't those the same lights you put up a week or so ago?"

The Newfie admitted they were.

"What did you pay for them," asked Benjamin.

"Fifty bucks," was the reply.

"I guess they were on sale," Benjamin noted. "They're seventy five now. I need three and that's a bit too much."

Dave turned to the clerk at the lumber desk, who was already somewhat bewildered by the Newfoundlander's approach.

"Hey buddy," he said. "Me bud here needs tree of dem lights at fifty bucks each."

"He should have been here three weeks ago and he could have had them. Now the price is regular," responded the clerk.

"Nope! Nope! They're not," said Dave. "I got 'em fer fifty bucks and dats what 'e'll be payin'."

The clerk never even spoke to Dave. He merely turned to Benjamin and said, "Look, if I give you the lights for fifty will you get him out of here."

Benjamin readily agreed.

The bill paid, Dave and Benjamin headed for home to see if the lumber arrived. At one thirty, it did.

Dave and Benjamin began measuring, framing, sawing and pounding nails. They couldn't believe the reaction of the neighbors. It was as if a dinner bell had been rung. Neighbors came from all directions to see what was going on, spun on their heels and went back home, returning in an instant with hammers of their own.

In three hours, Storm had her deck, complete with railings.

Monday morning, Benjamin left for work feeling very proud of himself. He and the neighbors had accomplished something to make Storm happy that he would never have believed could be done. She had her deck. The work was over.

But it wasn't. He pulled into the driveway that evening only to be taken behind the house and handed a paint brush and can of stain. This deck wasn't finished until it was stained and Storm intended to finish it right now.

Reluctantly, Benjamin began to paint railings while Storm worked on the deck floor. It seemed everything he did was wrong. Storm criticized his technique, the amount of stain he put on the boards and even the amount that was going on his hands. He tried to improve his work but it didn't seem to matter. Nothing he did was up to his wife's expectations.

At last, Storm said the magic words.

"Ben," she said, "if you can't paint right, don't paint at all."

She caught Benjamin on the upstroke. He calmly finished the stroke, opened his hand and let the paint brush pass over his shoulder and fall to the ground. There it lay as he walked away. His career as a painter was over.

Lorriane Fee

Chris did as he was taught. He shot high

Soccer Champion

The drive was short, the speech was long. But that is what can happen when your Dad is a coach, even if it isn't for your team. To take in all the advice, was not expected. Chris was young, eight years old, and hadn't shown a great deal of running ability on the soccer field, although he had listened to his Dad's tips in the past.

Noting ball handlers passing him on the field, Chris' Dad had informed him that there was a way to get the soccer ball. If he was to slide toward the ball carrier and check with his legs and feet, it was called a tackle and would serve the purpose. Chris had tired it, it worked and from then on he proved more effective on the field. He had also been shown how to play his position, rather than chasing the ball like a herd of stampeding buffalo and that too seemed to work.

But this morning was different. They were on their way to the city finals. It was the most important game they would play in the entire season. The Orange Crush was out to take home a trophy. They would crush their opposition.

"The goal posts are high and the goalie is short," the father said. "If you get a chance, shoot high. The goal tender will never be able to reach the ball and stop the shot."

The advice was sound. Now all that had to happen was to have an eight year old manage to kick the ball high. This, in itself, was a feat to challenge the child. Would he listen? Could he manage the kick? Only the game would show the answers.

From the opening kick off, the ball went to and fro on the pitch, chased by members of both teams. A herd of stampeding buffalo would have had far more order. Coaches screamed from the sidelines, giving instructions, attempting to get their team into some semblance of order. Nothing helped. The herd continued its stampeding.

Chris' Dad, however, held out hope. His son, designated to defense, remained out of the herd. He was following instructions and consistently swept the ball to the side whenever it approached the goal. He was doing his job.

At half time, with kids rushing to grab oranges and a pop, supplied by the parents, the Orange Crush coach decided to change his team's strategy and player positions. Nothing had been proven. The score was zero-zero.

"Chris," said the coach, "I want you to move up to forward and try to score."

With the beginning of the second half, Chris moved up, only to have disaster strike. With his absence, and for that matter the absence of any defender, the opposition scored a quick goal and went into the lead. Nonetheless, the Orange Crush coach stuck to his decision.

The stampede continued until an errant ball squirted loose from the herd. Chris was quick to jump to the advantage and headed for the goal, dribbling the ball in front of him. But just as he decided to take his shot, he was tackled from behind and knocked to the ground. His efforts would go without reward.

The whistle blew. The referee indicated there would be a penalty shot, one on one between Chris and the goaltender. All other players would wait until the stop was made or a goal was scored before joining the fray.

On command, Chris approached the ball and took his shot. It sailed far off the mark and harmlessly passed the goal without even challenging the goal tender. A chance to tie the game had been lost.

But wait! The referee indicated that the goalie had moved before the shot was taken. In spite of missing the goal entirely, a re-kick was awarded.

This time, Chris made no mistake. As young as he was, he knew where he went wrong on his first attempt. Remembering the coaching of his father, he took time to make the perfect shot and kicked the ball high. Untouched, it sailed into the net to tie the game.

Chris' father's chest expanded. "That's my boy. He's doing exactly what I told him," he told anyone who would listen.

Again the herd instinct took place. What were the boys thinking of? They were not only playing for a trophy and a championship. They were playing for oranges. The good guys were, after all, the Orange Crush.

In the dying second of the match, the ball again squirted loose from the pack and Chris pounced on it. With the herd in hot pursuit, he ran down the field, kicking the soccer ball along in front of him. The goal tender came out of his area to challenge the break away and Chris took his shot. It was high.

The shot was so high it seemed to go almost straight up. It didn't even reach the goal tender, but landed in front of him.

"That's it," the Orange Crush fans thought. "This game is going into a shoot out."

But it didn't. The ball finally found its way to earth, landed in front of the charging goal tender and bounced. It bounced high enough to be untouchable. Much to amazement of the parents, the ball bounced completely over the charging goalie and landed behind him. As he turned, all he could do is watch the ball trickle into the net for the winning goal and a championship for the Orange Crush.

Chris had followed his father's instructions and became the star of the day. The city championship belonged to the Orange Crush. Now, there was nothing left to do but head to the sidelines for more oranges.

Bucket Head

The best possible day is spent on a quiet lake, floating in a boat and dropping a fishing line over the side. With that criterion, this day promised to be the best of the best.

Loading themselves into the boat, the three fishermen jabbered excitedly as they set their rods and gear in appropriate places and prepared to cast off. What could get better than a quiet day on the lake, tucked away in the wilderness and surrounded by trees? With the exception of the loons that floated quietly on the water, this was their day and theirs alone.

The boat motor coughed to life and the craft began to move forward. Lines were dropped and the day's activities began in earnest. Father, son and uncle were prepared for the big hit. They knew the lake and its quirks and certainly knew where the fish would lie, basking in the sun, just beneath the surface.

Within moments the boy, Dan, was struggling with his line. In spite of being a big boy for the age of twelve, he had a battle on his hands. Fishing line pulled from the reel as his quarry ran away from near the boat. Slowly, Dan managed to get it close to the boat but each time, the huge trout would take line and make another run. After several runs, exhaustion took over and the net finally captured the fighting king of the lake. A moment to admire the catch and over the side it went, back to its basking.

It had been decided prior to departure that this would be a day devoted strictly to catch and release. Perhaps the fish were injured slightly by the hook and tired by the battle but there was no intent to end their lives. The fishermen were after the big one and, should they decide fish was on the dinner menu, the smaller fish would be tastier. Until then, all would be put back in the water.

Passing through narrows, which joined two sections of the lake, Dan's line tugged again.

"Another one," he chuckled as his fish broke the water and danced on its tail.

"Keep the line tight," his uncle Ben warned. "This one is even bigger."

Setting his own rod aside to control the boat for the expected landing, he heard his brother-in-law Mickey, give a hoot of joy.

"Got one too," he exclaimed and another trout broke the water to contribute its talent and do its dance.

With his hands full controlling the boat with two fish on lines, Ben did not notice his own rod.

"Grab the rod," yelled Mickey. "It's goin' in the lake."

A desperate grasp caught the end of the rod to secure it, only to warn Ben he too had a fish on line. Three fish to fight was beyond belief and brought about the need to shut down the boat engine and allow the boat to float as the three fishermen fought for their prizes.

The struggle over, fish landed, it was time to look once again to gaining control of the boat. While unattended, it had floated to the centre of the lake.

For the first time, the trio noted the lake was quiet no longer. Waves had begun to splash the sides of the boat. A wind had risen and, as is often the case with a shallow lake, it had become angry without warning.

The wind increased its velocity and dark clouds gathered overhead.

Suddenly, hailstones began to fall from the sky, pummeling the boat and those aboard.

"Hang on!" Ben yelled over the wind and hailstones pounding the boat. "We have to head for shore and the campsite's too far. I'll put the boat under those spruce trees on the nearest shore and we'll have to wait this out. At least we'll be away from the hail."

Mickey, worried about the welfare of his son, reached down for an ice cream bucket and put it over his son's head to protect him from the hail. With the handle tucked under his chin and a smile on his face, Dan appeared ready to battle the storm and any other strife which would come his way. Long live the knight.

Saying nothing, Ben put the boat up on shore and the group took refuge.

The storm passed as quickly as it had arrived and the boat and passengers began to make their way across the lake and back to camp. Not only were they pleased to return but their ladies who had waited and wondered were pleased to see their men healthy, if not happy.

Dan marched into camp grinning, his war helmet still in place. He had tackled the elements and emerged unscathed. But he wanted it to be as obvious as possible to the onlookers that he was prepared.

Ben's wife, Storm, observed Dan, in his armor, broke into a chuckle and asked, "Dan, why do you have Ben's pee bucket on your head?"

The response was surprise.

"You're kidding, right?" replied the boy.

"No!" came the last answer in the world Dan wished to hear. "Ben uses it when we're on the lake and then dumps it when we get back to camp."

With one motion, the war helmet landed in the bushes beside the camp. Dan was now unsure whether he had won or lost the battle, not to mention the war.

"Ah," said Ben. "Don't worry too much about it. I always rinse it."

Stealin' Time

For the pair of twelve year olds, it was their first major trip away from home. Asked by Chris' parents, his friend John was invited to experience Hawaii. They, of course, faced sharing a bed between them and sharing a room with Chris' parents.

It was an amicable trip with both boys taking an exact amount of spending money and each being offered the same opportunities. When Chris was given a boogy board to ride the waves, John took his choice of boards as well. All was to be equal.

There were, of course, some instances of inequality under the surface that would never be known to John. When their son was short on spending money but wanted a special souvenir, Chris' parents bought it and hid it in their luggage to give it him upon their return home. When John found underwater goggles on the beach, the pair shared until negotiations determined that Chris should have a pair of his own. Thus both boys were allowed to view fish in the rocks together. One pair of goggles and two snorkels were purchased. Now they could not only watch the fish but talk about them.

With the passing days, John began calling Chris' parents Mom and Dad. It was to avoid home sickness, of course, but Chris reacted with jealousy. He became even angry at every little thing that would occur.

Looking at his son, Chris' father said, "You and I have better have a little talk," and took his son outside. John wanted to join them but was discouraged. This was a private matter and not a 'social function'. Chris and Dad went alone. Where did they go? On a cruise of Honolulu in a rented mini jeep. Chris had to learn that he was, indeed, special. Regardless of what John called his Dad, he was his Dad's only son when the chips were down. For two hours the pair cruised before returning to their room where John was led to believe there had been a serious discussion regarding behavior.

Touring the island of Oahu proved to be the first error in judgment. Everyone enjoyed the ride in the little topless jeep, until the next day. Both boys, sitting high in the back awoke wind burned. A pair of red faced lobsters peered from under the sheets, complaining strenuously of sore faces. The parents could only hope their guest, John, turned out to have a tan upon arrival home. This would be a tough issue to explain to his parents.

The main interest on the island for the twelve year olds seemed, however, not to be the sights or activities it offered. On visiting a dancing display, one was given a lei by a dancer, the other was not. But in spite of their charms, these were old women to the boys. They wanted to meet girls.

On a warm tropical evening around the pool in the hotel, it happened. The two boys went off swimming without supervision and met the ladies of their dreams. A touring group of fourteen year old girls in Hawaii for a baseball tournament appeared. Outnumbering the only males in the pool, Chris and John, the girls showed interest. As for Chris and John, they did what any boy would do. They lied about their age and jumped at the opportunity to socialize with 'older women'.

The boys learned where the girls were staying in the hotel and as luck would have it, four were in the room adjacent to their own. The date was set. They had no supervision and invited the boys to join them later. This would require sneaking out as Chris was certain his parents would never agree to any request of this nature.

Assuming the parents were asleep, the two boys began to chat about their plans.

"Are they asleep yet?" John whispered.

"I think so. Now we can go next door and join the girls. Be quiet," was Chris' response.

Quietly the boys made their way out of the room and into the hallway discussing who had a key for their return. Little did they know, Chris' father laid awake, merely pretending sleep.

He felt no cause for worry. He knew where the boys were going and would stay awake to monitor the situation through the adjoining walls.

Two hours passed and he heard the door to the room open. Just as his two charges turned back the sheets and prepared to re-enter their bed, the father switched on a night light by his bed and looked at the boys. The pair froze.

"Well," he said. "Did you have a good time with the girls?"

There was no response from the other bed, just a pair of red faced twelve year olds who slipped quietly beneath the bed sheets and wondered what the morning would hold.

Lorriane Fee

He longed to go four by fouring in his new Jeep

Jeepers Creepers

It was to be a special holiday for Benjamin Bratt and his wife Storm. Plans for this holiday had been made and revamped each year for sixteen years. Now the time had come and the holiday was on. At last, they would have a holiday strictly for themselves as their child was finally old enough to stay home alone for a week or so.

Safety precautions had been taken. Their son had been given the normal list of do's and don'ts but along with it came a phone number. Benjamin had a mobile phone in his car and it was to be called if there were any problems at home whatever. The pair may not be able to get home quickly but could certainly contact someone near for help.

Sights were set on Deadwood, South Dakota. It was a healthy drive but distance didn't matter on this outing. They were determined to return to the state of being a young couple. There would be no motor home, no trailer. No siree! This time they would return to their roots, travel fast and sleep in a tent.

The plan seemed sound enough, especially when they bent the rules of camping and found their meals in restaurants. Even as they pulled into Great Falls, Montana for their first romantic night out, they were confident in their plan. This outing would rekindle a spark which had been lost over the years with family commitment.

There on the horizon, lit brightly for all to see, were the two signs they wanted; a café and a welcoming KOA campground.

Problems began with the KOA. There was limited tenting space provided and the pair found themselves tenting on a boulevard, with traffic circling them throughout the night. This could have been avoided had they called ahead and reserved a spot, or if they had their camper. There were camper spaces available but nothing for tents. Benjamin found himself reminded of his poor planning throughout supper and the early evening.

Supper over and the tent erected, Benjamin decided it was his turn and did his best to live up to the name of Bratt.

"I wonder how good the drivers are here?" Benjamin joked. "We're sitting in the middle of a traffic circle with no protection. I wonder if they'll even see this little tent?"

With those words, he turned over in his sleeping bag, smiled and drifted off to dreamland.

For Storm, however, his words made sense and pushed a panic button. On awakening in the morning, the first thing Benjamin noticed was Storm, laying on her back, eyes wide open and staring at the top of the tent as traffic roared outside. One night's sleep shot, as she wanted to see her end coming should a driver lose control and come crashing through the tent. She was awaiting her demise.

A side trip to Jackson Hole, Wyoming proved somewhat better. Visiting Old Faithful was part of the plan. However, it was somewhat disappointing to learn that the fabled geyser was about as consistent as Storm's temper. It erupted, but not every hour on the hour. It could vary by minutes and was totally unpredictable.

Camping facilities offered did seem to make up for other inconsistencies with grassy tenting areas close to the washrooms. On a beautiful August evening, the pair settled into their sleeping bags, Storm intent on catching up on lost sleep.

Although Benjamin was noted for finding an Achilles heel, he was determined to keep his comments to himself and allow Storm to catch up on some 'zzz's'. Mother Nature had different ideas, however. When he awoke, there lay Storm on her back, staring at the top of the tent with her teeth chattering. It was no wonder. Crawling out of his own bag and exiting the tent, the morning that greeted Benjamin was so cold, an inch of ice was found in a water bucket he had fetched the night before.

Deadwood, Mount Rushmore, South Dakota, lay before them. This day, they would reach their destination. These promised to be warmer and, perhaps by nightfall, Storm would finally thaw out.

According to Storm's wishes, the first search was for a campground. But Deadwood hosted only one—another KOA. The prices were unreasonable and there was no tenting area whatever. The only available property was on a gravel RV area. Learning there was a natural campground, without facilities, fifteen miles to the south, nothing else would live up to Storm's expectations.

It was little wonder. The scenery was breathtaking, with towering pines throughout and grassy tenting sites. And they had it all to themselves. Storm was beside herself with joy when she thought of the success of her decision.

Settling in their sleeping bags for the night, Storm noted the whisper of the wind in the trees.

"Doesn't it just lull you to sleep?" she asked Benjamin.

Benjamin had to admit the sound seemed to rejuvenate the soul. But before inviting sleep and dreams for a restful night, he posed questions, based on his observations.

"How tall do you think those trees are?" he asked his partner.

Her reply was non committal.

"How should I know?" she said. "Pretty tall."

"Do you think the wind will get any stronger?" Benjamin asked. "I think I heard thunder. There may be a storm coming in."

There was no response so he continued.

"Do you suppose any of these trees ever fall, maybe get hit by lightning?"

Again there was no response from his wife.

"If one fell, do think it would get hung up on another tree or just come crashing down, maybe on the tent?"

Storm had heard quite enough. An abrupt "Good Night!" ended the questioning.

Once again, Benjamin turned over in his sleeping bag intent on a good night's sleep. Once again, he awoke in the morning to find Storm staring at the top of the tent and waiting for the inevitable cracking sounds as a tree came crashing down on the couple's accommodations.

At last Storm found what she was searching for. They had come to Deadwood for two purposes, although they varied with the individual. For Benjamin, it was history and all it had to offer; Calamity Jane, Wild Bill Hickock, General Custer, Sitting Bull. It seemed endless. For Storm, it was one armed bandits. She had come to gamble and gamble she would.

Fortunately, with her preoccupation for the activity, she chose only nickel machines and won more often than not. But it made her happy. It was the activity, not the amount won or lost that held importance for her.

In spite of an excellent day and being tired from loss of sleep, she was not about to return to any wilderness campground when bedtime arrived and the KOA remained full.

"OK," they finally agreed. "We'll put the seats back and sleep in the car in a parking lot."

Just as Storm closed her tired eyes, Benjamin had two more questions.

"Do you think we're allowed to sleep in a parking lot like this?" he asked and went on to question the outcome of their actions. "Do you think the sheriff will come along and give us a ticket or just put us in jail for vagrancy?"

There was no reply from Storm in the passenger seat.

When he awoke next morning, somewhat cramped, Storm was sitting upright, bleary eyed and looking straight through the car's windshield in search of the lawman who was coming to take her away.

Realizing it was her last day, her last opportunity, perhaps her last minute to gamble, Storm ignored breakfast and headed for her favorite one armed bandit. She was in search of the triple sevens that would declare her a winner.

By afternoon, Benjamin had had enough and was drained of nickels and opted for a drink. Storm, however, was smiling with a bucket of nickels on her lap, more in the machine's trough and a sore arm from pulling handles. She was in heaven.

Suddenly, sheer pandemonium broke loose. Bells rang, sirens blew, lights flashed and Storm was shouting.

"Look! I won a jackpot! I won eight hundred nickels."

As he realized it was true, Benjamin dropped his head slightly. He couldn't look and didn't want to hear the answer to the question he was about to pose.

"How many nickels did you play?" he asked.

"Just one, but I won eight hundred!" was Storm's jubilant reply.

"Remember," Benjamin went on, "I've always told you to play the maximum on a progressive machine?"

"Sure! But I won a jackpot!"

"And look what you would have won if you'd just played the maximum," Benjamin said, pointing at a flashing arrow leading directly to a shiny new Jeep Renegade.

For some reason the trip home was rather silent. Benjamin seethed for a short time, considering offering his wife the opportunity to walk then settled down to pretending he was four-by-fouring in his new jeep.

For her part, Storm was doing what she had done throughout the trip, staring quietly into space and waiting for tragedy to strike.

About the Author

Growing up in a farming community without modern facilities in the '40s and '50s, it was common place for children to entertain themselves through reading or listening to their elders tell tales of the past. At a very early age, Jay Bernard discovered he had the gift of story telling and soon joined the group. Even the seasoned story tellers agreed he could wind a good tale.

This is Jay Bernard's second book. **Life's a Laughin' Matter** is a collection of stories recounting Jay's many adventures while spending his teenager's years at the farm, then in school, in the army reserves, and finally as a married man with a son of his own. The entertainment never ceases when considering that **Life's a Laughin' Matter.**

Jay can certainly spin a very good yarn!

Printed in the United States
46118LVS00003B/118-141